To Liz

CW00616644

# Yours Truly,

# Brian

## and Other Stories

Serena Diss

First published 2013
By Rowanvale Books
57, Brynllwchwr Road,
Loughor,
Swansea
SA4 6SQ
www.rowanvalebooks.com

A CIP catalogue record for this book is
available from the British Library.
ISBN 978-0-9574934-8-3

To
DONAL
without whom

How do I know what I think
till I see what I say.

E. M. Forster

# ACKNOWLEDGEMENTS

My gratitude to Dr. Kathy Hopewell (Bangor University) who first urged me to publish.

Thank-you Sarah and Karen for all your encouragement and support.

I am grateful to Shay Daly who made some valuable observations in the final stages.

My thanks to Sarah and Cat (Rowanvale Books) for being so prompt and responsive.

# Yours Truly, Brian

## and Other Stories

Serena Diss

# CONTENTS

# YOURS TRULY, BRIAN

## The Accident - Miriam

Miriam pours herself a gin and martini.  She confides in the photograph of an elderly lady watering an orchid-type plant on the windowsill which always seemed to look rather rude.

Oh, Mother! This is what I need. I don't know if I'm coming or going.  It's the shock of seeing him. His head and face were such a mess. He couldn't really talk - I think his eyes seemed to be smiling.

I brought in his pyjamas and toiletries but I found him in a green gown. I asked if he'd come back from the operating theatre. They said no; he'd had x-rays and other things and they were monitoring him. Then they asked would I take his clothes home as they hadn't facilities for keeping them in the hospital. I thought how heartless is that! It's like collecting the belongings of someone who has passed away! They assured me he wasn't in pain, the medical staff, and as far as I could make out amongst all the bandaging he seemed…umm… positive, so anyway I chatted on.

'I've rung your office. I've told them you'd had an accident and you probably wouldn't be in for the next few days… The car's a write off.' I thought he might as well know, though he didn't seem to be taking anything in, so I decided I'd better not add that it's still stuck down the canal bank upside-down for everyone to gawp at!

Of course, they'll all be gossiping about it - nobody misses anything in our street. Things haven't changed, Mother; it's amazing how information can travel. You can bet your life Marjorie Finnick is the number one messenger. Remember Marjorie? She's as nosey as ever was. I can't decide if it's her geriatric imagination or she's just that touch spiteful. Anyways, she's got it in for me - or Brian.

'Your husband's got a long lost niece, or a bit on the side, Miriam. He drops her off every week at the traffic lights y'know.'

I feel I can't be too nowty with her, her husband's inside for aggravated burglary. I must say he never struck me as an aggravated burglar.

A few weeks back when I got caught up in the hose Brian was using to wash the car, he shouted could I switch it off at the wall. I ended up drenched and twisted my ankle. As I stumbled to the front door she came running across the road.

'I heard your husband shouting at you something terrible, Miriam, and you're limping. What's he done to you? I'd report him, me y'know.' So that's Marjorie for you.

I'd better get the insurance papers out of the V.I.P. box… I suppose. I can't help thinking however did the car end upside-down? It's a mercy *he* didn't end up in the canal. Brian's such a good driver; he's never had any points on his license. I wonder how the ambulance people got him out? I'll wait while tomorrow, he'll tell me then - visiting time two o'clock. I can get the number twelve bus.

* *

I must sit down a bit. I've had such a peculiar afternoon. It was Brian. I can't fathom it all out - oh don't worry, Mother, he's alright - but I felt I had to busy myself fighting with that telescopic umbrella before taking a good look at him. His face was quite bruised. It must be sore. He'd

3

had it stitched. I said he was looking much better than I thought he would. I think he tried to smile… I waited but he didn't seem in the mood to chat – it'll be the stitches. I expect they have to pull the skin together rather tight… It's difficult to talk to Brian sometimes; I don't quite know what to say. Anyway, I put my hands round my knees to aid conversation and then I started.

'One good bit of news, Brian - the telly's fixed. The boss engineer came this time. He didn't want to go into the loft when I said I thought we had a rat or a squirrel up there and to mind the traps. But when I told him you were in hospital he took pity on me and went up. He fiddled with the aerial and now I can see *The World's Strongest Man* on a summer's afternoon instead of in a snowstorm!' I laughed at that and he managed a sort of one-sided grin.

Then I described my ideas for re-furbishing the downstairs and he agreed it would freshen things up. You know, he didn't say anything about the colour scheme I'd planned. I thought he might, since he goes to history of art classes, but whatever. I said 'the accident money is the silver lining, as the saying goes.' Then he perked up.

'The accident money?'

'Yes,' I told him, and there were all sorts of insurances and I'd bring in the papers now he was on the mend. Then his mouth seemed to relax and after a bit, quite out of the blue, he said couldn't I forget about the housekeeping for a while and we could spend some of it on a tour or a trip abroad somewhere.

'A tour? A trip?' I was gobsmacked! I wonder if I could cope with something like that? I wasn't exactly…over the moon about it. It's all so sudden and so confusing. He's never mentioned anything about a tour before. Anyway, he assured me I'd love it and eased up in the bed and got really chatty. He had it all worked out! It was to be Corfu - a Greek island.

'Think of it, Miriam,' he said. 'The heat, the sapphire-blue Ionian sea, crystal-clear water, drifting along the coast and mooring our boat at the harbour tavernas for lunch,' - which seemed to be fried goats' cheese and other Greek food I can't remember the name of. He gave me this book by Gerald Dur-r-ell or something.

'We can actually eat in his house,' he said. 'It's now a taverna. What do you think?'

I didn't' know what to think. *Myself and Other Animals*? What did he give me this for? I wonder what *he's* thinking of? Oh, I've got an awful gnawing sensation inside…

'Brian,' I started - but then at that point the tea-trolley rattled down the ward and I felt so relieved that now wasn't the right moment to try and get out what I wanted to say. I'll raise it tomorrow. Yes. Number twelve bus, one thirty – five.

* *

Marjorie's right. There *is* someone else. I saw the ambulance crew and asked them had they attended to Brian Boothroyd two nights ago and they said they had.

'He and the young lady were lucky. Saved by their seat belts, they were.'

'Young lady?'

'Yes, she went home yesterday. She doesn't want to bring any charges. He's still in - banged up his head a bit. D'you know him?'

'I think so... I'm his wife...' I was caught properly surprised. Was this my Brian? Who was she? He'd been to his history of art class – hadn't he? But it's not anywhere near the canal. I'll not let on anything yet, I decided, as I climbed up to the ward on the first floor.

Then I suddenly had a vision of the pair of them suspended upside-down by their sea-belts in the car on the canal bank, and I started to laugh. I couldn't help it. Such a comical image struck me, I laughed louder...and louder... I couldn't stop. A doctor coming down the stairs asked if I was alright!

Anyway, while I was in that agitated state of mind it seemed the golden opportunity to raise it with Brian. Of course it wasn't golden - what's golden about your husband taking up with someone else? But it was the opportunity, feeling like I was, to bring it into the open. But I didn't feel exactly 'open' either. In fact, I began to feel more and more closed the nearer I got to the top of the stairs. I came straight out with it:-

'Brian, I saw the ambulance crew when I came into the hospital, the ones who brought you in…'

And I told him about the young woman who'd left the hospital yesterday. He actually seemed relieved, somehow. We never really shared much of the deeper things of life, our relationship (I don't like the word 'relationship', it's too…heavy), but he seemed to want to get it off his chest.

'I met her in the art class. We studied paintings…then we stayed on a bit and compared ideas…and had something to eat. We tried a different continental meal each week. Then we went to some art galleries sometimes. I was taken with all the vibrant colours, the culture and…the exuberance of it all. It made me… It made me …'

He stopped and couldn't say anything else. Neither of us could say anything else.

I was so afraid of all the things that he might be thinking - that he had felt dead, and she made him feel alive again, or our life at home had got so dreary and boring, and the art classes showed him what he was missing, or being with someone young and, what was it? 'exuberant', gave a new meaning to life - but he didn't say any more.

We just sat there.

Eventually he asked me had I thought any further about Corfu, and then the penny dropped. It was obvious: the trip had actually been planned with the other woman. It was all too well arranged - the book about the animals, the boat trips, and tavernas, and everything.

After a bit I spoke.

'Brian, I'm not the student woman from the art class. Do you really want to take *me* to Corfu?'

There was a pause that seemed to last ages.

'Yes, Miriam'.

'It won't be the same.'

'I know.'

'I don't know if I can match up to second best.'

Then he said what I'd been waiting for, for so long. What I'd given up hope waiting for.

'I know what I've done, and I'm sorry. I want you to know it is *you* I love, Miriam.'

Yes, he said that.

'I love you, Miriam.'

He talked about different kinds of love - companionship and all that, and… 'other things can mellow given time, if we let them.'

I knew what he was wanting to talk about. He watched me as I closed my hands round my knees and I had the oddest sense of wanting to be invisible … of wanting to leave a note saying 'How can I be like that anymore?' in the empty milk bottle on the doorstep.

Then I said, 'I love you too, Brian. Let's go to Corfu.'

He reached out to me and I… I smoothed his patched-up face.

\* \* \*

# YOURS TRULY, BRIAN

## The Accident - Avril

It's the end. It's the end of the dream trip to Corfu, and I'm really gutted big time. I feel cheated, especially as this surgical collar is so stupid and uncomfortable propping up my aching, anguished neck. That's it - I'm anguished. I'm anguished because I can't turn my head sideways and it could take weeks to get right.

Look at yourself, Avril - the jilted mummy! But why do I feel so guilty? There's nothing to feel guilty about. His embrace came quite out of the blue - while he was still at the wheel! Why did he *do* that? Could he, maybe, have been carried away by Klimt's picture of *The Kiss* we were poring over in art class? Could he have wanted to surprise me with some kind of wild spontaneous release of pent-up emotion? Did he want me to know he loved me? Whatever it was, if he'd just pulled on the hand-brake, passion or no passion, the car wouldn't have careered down the canal bank and ended up on its roof.

If only he'd stopped the car and then when we'd taken off our seat belts - oh, what then? What I've been waiting for. What I've been longing for… As it turned out, he got my seat belt off after a gruelling struggle and then banged his head getting *his* off as he hit the roof. Then the fire-brigade arrived!

Now I'm just stiff and drained and dried up.

'You'll be glad to know it's nothing more than whiplash,' they said in A&E. Glad?  That's rich!  It's almost a relief to shut the door on the whole incident… accident… I mean, episode… Oh, it's the whole dream I had of our romantic adventure on a sun-soaked Greek island!

Brian isn't - wasn't - like other men. He was starry-eyed, kind of out-of-this-world. He had this obsession to know everything about the artists, and marvelled at some of the paintings we saw in the galleries. How he swept me along with his enthusiasm, and I marvelled too. I was on cloud nine in his company because he was so different and so genuine.

I nearly bumped into his wife last night in the hospital. I was going into his ward to see if he was OK and I saw the back of her sitting at his bedside. She's bound to cotton on now. It could even get into the papers.

Looking back, my dream was just a bubble, a fragile, swelling, glowing bubble that floated into my space with a promise of everything exciting and new. And now the bubble has burst. Oh - ouch! Oh God, my neck! I'm hurting so! Oh, where's my handkerchief? I can't stop crying...

The other men were married too, and always amounted to 'hubby with an eye for a bit on the side'. To put it crudely, instead of tucking into roast beef and Yorkshire and bread-and-butter pudding, they'd fancy tucking into salmon-en-croûte and pineapple pavlova - and that's where I came in. They were only interested in grunting and groping with the appetites of the flesh, never with a taste for the higher things in life, like our history of art classes.

*They'll* stop too now, of course. That's the end of art history, it'll have to be. I'll always link Klimt and that with Brian, even though he won't be there again. Now I'll have to drum up an interest in something else I suppose... I wonder what 'Antiques and Collectables' is like?

* *

I feel good. I'm a new woman now my neck brace has gone, and I do like Brendan. Mirror, mirror, on the wall, is he the fairest of them all? He signed up for the 'Antiques and Collectables' course the same night as me. He's a wheeze! He's Irish. Now how does his accent go?

'I'll not kid you, the real pull is making a bit o' money, but you need to know your spitoon from your chamber-pot said the priest who was caught short driving Reverend Mother on retreat.'

'Have you got a shop then?'

'No, I'm one of McAlpine's fusiliers.'

'Come again?'

'I work on construction sites, but I buy antiques and take 'em to Ireland and sell 'em. It's a hobby. You should give it a go, Avril.'

Brendan isn't curious like Brian. He's interested to learn how you can date a piece of furniture. He's even more interested in how to judge a fake or a 'marriage' as they call it, but he wouldn't go overboard about the carving or patina or the provenance of the piece. Brian would have been really into that.

He wanted me to go to an auction at St. Peter's church hall. He'd got this idea of buying up stuff and we'd take it to Ireland. We'd get the boat from Holyhead.

'Sure to God I know the Shannon area like the back of me hand - we'd do the Athlone- Birr- Nenagh run. I've a nose for the places where they'll jump at Belleek figurines, Doulton tea-sets, Edwardian kitchenware and the like. How about it, Avril?'

He's married, or hitched-up, or semi hitched-up. There's a boy… or a girl.

'I'll think about it, Brendan. I'll come to the auction.'

'Do, and the best deal on the HSS is the long weekend four-day return.'

The dearest items I bid for were described in the list as a pair of Imari models of dogs with comical faces, and a pottery 'stick man' figure which reminded me of Lowry. They cost me over two hundred and fifty pounds, but Brendan's sure we can make a profit of at least forty per cent.

On Monday I faced up to the office dragon.

'Avril, you've already been off work for three weeks with neck-ache.'

'Whiplash.'

'…and now it's time off for a funeral on Friday and an outpatients' appointment next Monday. I'd call that sailing close to the wind, wouldn't you? Particularly as you're hardly IT literate, which was required in the job spec-ification. I shall have to speak to the manager, Mr. Robotham, about it.'

She did, and it's my last chance, he said. 'So make the most of it.'

He must have guessed something!

However, on the Wednesday before the long weekend I had this weird dream. It was so real it was uncanny. It was like an omen.

We were going up a ramp to the top deck of the ferry and I was getting nervous as Brendan's van is a bit of a banger. He sensed I was and put his hand on my knee and winked. Then he gave me a sexy once-over on the steepest bit of the ramp and suddenly had to put his foot down. He drove straight into the back of the Merc in front. The rear doors of the van flew open and, in amazement, I watched all the Doulton tea-sets, Belleek china, my dogs with comical faces, cruets, spitoons, chamber-pots, condiment-sets and cutlery tumbling down the ramps under all the cars, wrappings flying in all directions, and the whole lot disappeared into the sea.

My first thought when I woke up, in a sweat, was *Oh God, not another accident! First Brian and now Brendan. If ever there's an ominous wake-up call, this is it, Avril.*

I had to break the bad news to Brendan.

'I can't go to Ireland, I'll lose my job if I do. I'm ever so sorry, Brendan.'

So, now here I am staring at the dogs with comical faces and the rest of the stuff I'm saddled with, and I realise, quite suddenly, that I *want* to lose my job. I want to lose my job and not have anything to do with married men, or two-timing men, or even single men, come to that. What I really want is to do a proper course of study, one that leads to a career I'll be happy with, in the arts maybe. It will fill my life and I'll feel I'm making a contribution of *me*, myself, and can make my mark *really*, and not just be dreaming. Maybe then, it could be I'll meet someone like Brian, who is free.

\* \* \*

## YOURS TRULY, BRIAN

### The Accident - Brian

The pit and the pendulum… The pit and the… He couldn't make sense of anything, put anything together. The pendulum swung over the water, coming nearer and nearer, propelling him mercilessly towards the pit. He was in agony.

There was a woman, then the pain blotted her out, then his face stretched taut on the rack, ratcheting tighter and tighter.

'Don't leave me on the rack, Avril,' he spluttered. Their lips had met at last in a consummate kiss, then the crash in his head and everything spinning, the car spinning towards the canal.

'We're going to drown! Help! Help, someone! H-E-L-P!'

'Haven't you managed to get to sleep yet, Mr. Boothroyd? You'll wake all the patients… It's delayed shock, isn't it? Hush, calm down. Let me have your arm. Now, a little prick, it's just something to make you sleep.'

* *

'Cup of tea, Brian? … Mr Boothroyd, are you ready for your tea? You'll manage it through this straw. Let's plump up the pillows. That's it, and we'll tidy up the bandaging before your wife comes this afternoon. Cheer up! You'll be eating in no time.'

As he sucked through the straw Brian pieced together the terrifying events as they came back to him bit by bit.

'What's happened to Avril'?

'Oh, she went home last night after they'd fitted her with a neck-brace. She popped into the ward to ask after you. Your wife was with you so she said, under the circumstances, she'd never come again.'

So - it was the BIG 'E'. He felt utterly bereft. All that remained was pay-back time for what he wryly acknowledged could be interpreted as philandering, though it had never seemed like that with Avril. Some of his colleagues in 'Sales' had got away with it - or said they had - and here *he* was in 'Accounts' with only pain and a potentially public humiliation, and he had lost Avril.

All that was left was the cost. At the last count it amounted to £500 for the flight, £750 for the villa with swimming pool and front-line-sea-views, plus a wodge of 1,000 euros - and a hopeful packet of condoms.

And his face! How could he ever bear to look at himself in the mirror? He'd always thought he had OK looks, even better than OK - tallish, broadish, a good head of hair, greying at the sides a bit, but distinguished, and dark-hazel eyes.

'You're a deep one,' people used to say. But now he was a broken man with a cracked jaw and stitched up head and face - properly stitched up! My God, even Miriam would baulk at that!

\* \*

Brian watched his wife battle with her dodgy umbrella then launch into catch-up time. When Miriam felt awkward she always talked a lot. Some people clam up, others chatter on; she was one of those.

He wondered how much she knew about his accident. The nursing staff were bound to have gleaned the gory details but it was unlikely she'd know anyone from the hospital. After a bit she spoke of all sorts of insurances she'd found from what she called the V.I.P. box - 'accident money', as she put it.

Suddenly he shot up in the bed. That's it! He could cover all the bills - only he'd be taking Miriam rather than Avril to his dream island on his dream holiday. He looked at her, his kind, dependable, house-proud wife, and his heart wept.

How could he recapture the woman he first knew, so fresh and unencumbered with the day-to-day? He'd found her at that brief moment in time when she saw all the endless possibilities in life coming together in their love. She was quite open and free then to say and do what she really wanted and felt. He blurted out his proposition of the trip.

Miriam was amazed, as he guessed she would be, and could barely take in the suggestion. He gave her Gerald Durrell's book about Corfu, *Myself and Other Animals,* and she left the ward staring at it in bewilderment. Then he was suddenly overcome with concern for her. Would she get the number 12 bus alright? She'd be alone. She'd be lonely. At that moment he had an overwhelming desire to be with her.

Of course Miriam learned about Avril. She'd quizzed an ambulance crew and they'd put her fully in the picture. She was strangely quiet when he explained about the places they'd seen and the meals out.

She listened rather wistfully, then rather in wonderment when he told her how he really loved *her*. He stretched out his arms to reach her - she stroked his patched-up face - and he realised it would take time to convince her he truly did.

\* \*

Things were changing. Brian had started sketching the man in the opposite bed. He wished he wasn't always masking his face with the *Sporting Post*, or lying sideways. Eventually the man asked Brian to pop out to the corridor and buzz William Hill's for him.

'I'll tell you what, I'll ring in your bets if you'll put down your paper and sit still, in a frontal position, for a bit, so I can have a go with your face,' Brian replied.

'You're on,' he grunted.

The following morning he surveyed the drawing of himself and nodded.

'That's a good 'un. You've got the makings of an artist, me lad.'

'Thanks. Yes, thanks, you've done me a real favour saying that.'

And, there and then, Brian decided to take up classes in Life Drawing.

Oddly enough, Miriam had developed a new interest in paintings. She'd been to the City Art Gallery in Manchester and was especially taken with 'The Pre-Raphaelites in Their Time', Room 5. That was something of a surprise.

When Brian was ready to be discharged from the hospital, Miriam brought him the clothes he had asked for and added a base-ball cap to cover his head.

She looked at him now the bandages had been removed. His hair had been shaven where his head was stitched and she got a shock - it reminded her of when the cat had mange - but his face wasn't puffy anymore and the bruising had faded to yellow. Thankfully the scar on the right side wasn't as marked as she thought it might be.

He looked at her. She'd had her hair done back from her face now, and added bright red tints which glinted in the sun's rays. She was wearing a colourfully patterned dress which flowed, rather than being arranged in tight pleats.

'It's a William Morris design, do you like it?'

'You look stunning…' and he thought of the models in *their* flowing garments, perhaps even in no garments and he'd be sketching them in the Life Drawing classes.

* * *

# YOURS TRULY, BRIAN

## The Accident - Marjorie

Oh wonderful! On the front page of *The Rochdale Post,* there it is - Brian Boothroyd's car upside-down on t'canal bank and him with a young woman, the two of them clinging to the window for dear life! Oooh isn't he properly caught with his bit-on-the-side! What a laugh - it's made my day. Oh, I'll have to phone Madge and Florence and Janice with this one.

I'll hardly be able to resist a teeny-weeny bit of gloating when I tell Miriam 'I told you so', especially after *my* humiliation at Valley End Primary, bottom of main road. Seven years its lollipop lady, seven years! And I really liked that job. The kids always kept me up to date with the gossip and goings-on - it's amazing what they pick up - and Miriam's humiliation has brought it home, like.

It all happened when I was chatting to my 'Pips and Squeaks', as I used to call them, while we were crossing the road and that so-and-so 4-by-4 suddenly screeched to an emergency stop. Oh, I couldn't begin to repeat the vile language the driver used tearing me off a strip. The cheek of it - accused me of taking *my* eye off the job! And then… he drove into the school playground, barged into the Head's office and launched into a grossly exaggerated account of what happened which ended up as a major complaint. Thanks to him my nice little earner ended up hitting the buffers!

I do miss the children … If I'd had any of my own…but it wasn't to be - all miscarriages… and then…nothing, and you can't do owt about that so there's no use harping on.

Anyway, soon afterwards Florence's youngest, from number 25, nearly came a cropper didn't she? It's those tight skirts half-way up her b.t.m. - she was asking for it. Prop-os-itioned - yes that's it, propositioned she was by a kerb-crawler. I saw it all from 30 yards off. She did have the wit to scarper, but when I took the trouble reporting it to the community police, the silly girl didn't want to know! Notwithstanding, they said 'well why don't you start a neighbourhood watch scheme?' Why not, I thought, that's right up my street, so to speak.

I soon had the 'THIS IS A NEIGHBOUR-HOOD WATCH AREA' triangle attached to the telegraph pole outside our house and now I'm the co-ordinator, and I tell you there isn't much gets past my watch!

One thing I do keep an eye on is the jeweller's shop on the corner. There's a foreigner come to run it and he seems to hide his wife in the room at the back 'cause I've seen her peering round the door sometimes - and that's *all* I've seen of 'er.

He's put a white Persian cat in the middle of the window. It looks like a real one but it isn't, it's just a display with a diamond tiara on its head, a diamond necklace round its neck and two ruby bracelets on its feet.

My Dandy always barks like mad at it when we pass and I've complained to the man about it but he just stares at me. The locals call it 007 'cause it's just like the one in *Goldfinger* where the bad guy's got it sitting on his knee.

What really gets me is when he closes the shutters at night they catch its tail and it hangs limply from the bottom and people think it's a real cat's tail what's caught. I've told him about that too, but he just stares.

I've got to confess that I'm not actually the neighbourhood-watch co-ordinator any more.

It's my Eddie. He said he was bothered about the cat's tail hanging there and took his steel-cutter to the shutters one Sunday night to free it. Then the foreign man came out and grabbed him like, holding the tiara and bracelets and stuff.

My Eddie has a short fuse and he hit him with the steel-cutter which made him fall down. Then the woman from the back room sounded the alarm and the cops arrived.  They wrestled Eddie as he was trying to retrieve the cutter from the chap's arm as he was lying there on the pavement. They must have decided he was duffing him up 'cause he's now doing time for aggravating burglary - two years.

I miss 'im - I miss 'im, in spite of his drinking and temper and stuff. The house is empty…like me…. Anyway, the triangle's been moved to a telegraph pole at the bottom of the street, outside Mavis's house, so that's the end of that.

I've been trying to find out who was the woman in the car that Brian has taken up with, but the ambulance people won't tell me.

Miriam's standing by 'im - they came back from the hospital together. She's dyed her hair red and she had a right swanky dress on. They've got money from the car crash I bet. I don't think they should have it - not with him two-timing like that, but he's not the first one at it in this street and he won't be the last. There's plenty I could say, but my lips are sealed.

* * *

# BELINDA

He's on such good form today. It's a Holy Day of Obligation - St. Peter and St. Paul - and he's been to Mass. His God must be looking after him, something's working for him, Belinda thought, making him happy and really wanting to please. His God isn't the same as mine, it's much more real for him and I'm glad.

Belinda believed that the received view of getting old, or maybe the convenient view for the rest of the population, is that of golden years when you've only yourself to please, but she didn't find it like that. The life-long task of having someone else to please doesn't end when the someone else collects his retirement clock; it makes two with all the time in the world with only themselves to please.

She'd read in the paper about the problems of the people in Pakistan looking both ways, East to Islam and West to the democratic countries, and the terrible mess it was making of everything. She thought that, odd as it might seem, it could be compared to their conundrum of getting old, where the problem of what she and he can and can't do also grows into a muddle of looking both ways.

He can't walk without a stick so his progress is relaxed, but she needs the fast pace to keep up the flexibility in her hips, so while he goes south slowly up the fields, she goes briskly north over the bridge into the town. His arms are strong so he's in the garden. She finds lifting and pulling heavy stuff difficult, so she's in the house, and somehow they accommodate or capitulate to looking both ways. But could the Pakistanis do that? Maybe their problem is that they can't look back.

'I'm Irish to the bone, Belinda, but I'll not hold grudges about the old Empire now - that's history as far as I'm concerned. The IRA was Ireland's glorious resurrection and me uncle Dan drew his pension for the rest of his life with honour on it but those were the early days - he'd turn in his grave if he saw how it's ended up. The provos betrayed Ireland, so they did, and broke the heart of Roisin Dubh.'[1]

So Matt could look back, though, being of the older generation, for him there were only two realities: Hell and America. He was doing

---

[1] Roisin Dubh - Dark Little Rose, one of Ireland's famous political songs.

his best to discount the prospect of hell and had repressed from consciousness his urge to go to America, but she knew underneath it still lingered. There again it's the looking-both-ways conundrum - she can't face the prospect of flying and he can't acclimatise to going on his own, so while he looks wistfully westwards, first stop New York, she looks no further than the craggy Welsh coast with its dependable ebbs and flows, where she can stay put.

She was reluctant to admit that this muddle of opposites had brought something of a dilemma into their lives. He'd perhaps been over-optimistic in his views of retirement, so was the more surprised at the size of the gap between expectation and actuality.

Then, one evening -

'Belinda, I'm joining "The Sons of Rest"'.

It had an unpleasant impression of finality about it.

'Oh, Matt, what is it? Is it the doctor you've been to?'

'No, I've been in the *Rope and Anchor* with the other lads who've retired from the council and we've decided to form a social group.' That came as a welcome antidote to her function of trying to please and she was glad for him.

As time went on, the Sons of Rest enjoyed an enviable number of activities and trips, from a visit to the Llechwedd Slate Caverns, to pitch-

and-putt, a weekend at the Chester Races and another to Blackpool for the illuminations. Then there was a week in a narrow-boat, cruising from Llangollen Wharf. Drifting across Telford's Pontcysllte Aqueduct had long been his dream.

The climax to these increasingly ambitious programmes came a few months later when one Friday night he returned home with two large bunches of fragrant red carnations, her favourite flowers.

'Belinda, my girl, I've something really special to tell you tonight, so I have. Are you ready for this? The gang's arranging a visit to America - so, what do you think? Would you mind, would you?'

She didn't know what to think. He said it, triumphant at last, the opportunity of a lifetime, and he seemed so different that night, the flowers quite forgotten. He was the man she used to know, his face flushed and the smell of whisky on him and all, just like the days of old. I'm glad for him, she decided.

'How many of you are going?'

'Six at least. I'm not the only one with Irish relatives in Boston. They've a great feeling for the Irish over there so we'll not be lacking for the craic. It's for two weeks, Lindy, and flying out and back. Can I go?'

How long was it since he'd called her that? And there he stood, like a stripling boy asking for his pocket-money. How could she not be glad for him? But yet …

'Oh do, it's the chance of your life.' At this he seized her and swung her round and round in the kitchen till they tripped over the dog who was dizzily dodging after them as they held each other, catching each other's breath and finally collapsing into their chairs.

\* \*

She knew it was for the best when the great day came. He needed to get America out of his system, but as she waved them off she had a sinking feeling of wonder whether he would ever come back. She hadn't caught up with his new-found happiness and the weight of it made her feel thin, like a bow without a fiddle, like the air with no sound in it, like the oil-cloth on the table without the stain of his cup of tea. She was looking now only his way, across the Atlantic in the westerly sun, and a night chill was seeping in under the kitchen door. *I'm glad for him,* she reiterated.

Two weeks had nearly gone by before the long-distance phone call finally came. She hesitated, picking up the receiver.

'Is that you, Belinda?'

'Yes, how's the holiday been?'

'Great. I've an amount to tell you. You'll never guess, I've unearthed a cousin I never knew I had. Think of that! I'll have to keep the call short, but he's coming back over with me Lindy, to stay with us for a bit. He's nobody much left here, you know. Is that alright, is it?'

'Well, yes.'

'Good. He's called Eamonn.'

'Who?'

'Eamonn - you know…de Valera?'

'Who's that?'

'Never mind. He's a wealth of stories on him. You'll die laughing, so you will. My money's running out. Our flight's due back the day after tomorrow in the afternoon at half-past two… Are you there, Belinda?'

'Yes, I'll be there.'

'Great. "Here's looking at you, kid," as they say over here. Bye for now.'

The phone clicked and that was it. Was she glad? She didn't rightly know. The house had been empty…and draughty…but when the logs flamed up and the coals turned red it was cozy, quiet and easy.

A cousin. He has a few cousins and nephews and nieces. Oh, well, there'll be plenty of talking and activity soon enough she thought, and got out the rolling-pin, eggs and flour and her biggest bowl and sighed that she was glad for him.

# LOCKED OUT

I'm quite an easy person to accommodate, and can bed down like a nomad in unexpected places so long as there's *quiet*.

I've slept soundly many a night in the most makeshift of arrangements, if quintessentially quiet, whether in a B&B, a friend's pied-à-terre, or some little gem in the Dordogne.

I was once able to nod off in a broom-cupboard on the second floor of a four-star hotel in York, which, would you believe, overlooked platform 1 of the mainline station. (The brochure had only shown the south-facing aspect with a view of undulating lawns. I won't bore you with the details but if you're an insomniac you need to watch that one.)

I must acknowledge that the majority of my destinations had in common the facility to utilise an en-suite, or bathroom or, if needs must, a shower-room-cum-toilet as an emergency sleep-provider. Take, for example, the gem in the Dordogne. It had a shower-room converted from part of the landing, so no windows, so no shrill blast from a cockerel at dawn to demolish one's slumbers. (Please note, a disturbing upsurge of this cockerel sound-hazard is becoming more prevalent in rural France.)

On another occasion, a studio in Florence had a bathroom which allowed me to stretch out fully if my head was under the wash-basin and a foot each side of the toilet trunk. But, even there, an owl had a look-out on a pediment above - you've guessed it - the bathroom roof. It hooted full throttle through most of the witching hours and I wasn't above mentioning it in the guest-book at the end of our stay. Of course, it might lull a different sort of person to sleep and be a winner, you never know - winners and losers, winners and losers.

But there are some arrangements where one has to draw the line. You *do* need a room, be it ever so Lilliputian, with four walls and, ideally, without a window (clearly a rarity in any permutation) and which you have to yourself.

When I went to London for an occasion of special spiritual interest - the grandchildren's Confirmation by the Bishop of Southwark - I inhabited a kind of log-cabin-cum-office at the bottom of the garden, which everyone called "The Shed".

It's a no-brainer that if you have four children, five relatives, two dogs, two Siamese cats, a lop-eared rabbit and a hamster, all residing indoors, the possibility of *quiet*, even in some alcove or under-stairs repository, is out of the question - hence "The Shed".

Ah, and there's the rub. A row was beginning to gestate when the owner of "The Shed" (you can work it out, I don't like naming names) was not inclined to locate the key to the lock.

'It's not necessary, the office equipment hasn't required one and there are two top-of-the-range computers in there, plus a sound-system and other technical apparatus.' (Thinks: 'which you wouldn't understand'.) But I did, by implication, understand that a mere human couldn't possibly come to grief if all that expensive equipment had so effortlessly avoided any mishap.

Anyway, at the end of this day of Our Lord, when the Bishop of Southwark had done the honours, I swallowed a mogadon and crunched down on a camp-bed in this technological wonderland. After all, these Genie gadgets with their green and red winkers were keeping an eye out for anything untoward, and no birds sang.

In the early hours before dawn, my sleep was arrested by a rustling and a swishing and a creeping-through-the-bushes kind of noise. (Keep this critical moment on hold as I must briefly digress.) I have to concede that I could have made quite a decent stand and demanded the key to this shed. You may think, under the circumstances, I should have done so, but the fact of the matter is that I came to wonder if it was actually necessary.

I'm saying this because the door was a stable-door and I had noticed that the bottom part was incorrectly aligned so that the bolt mightn't marry-up to the door-frame catch, so even if the top *was* locked, the burglar, rapist, murderer or vagrant might only need to lower his head and step through the bottom half. Digression over - back to the terror that struck.

I tumbled out of the shed, stumbled up the crazy-paving path through the pigeon-droppings and slithered along steps to the kitchen back-door. Locked!! I dared to look back! A fox's bushy tail disappeared over the garden wall. I dumbly looked forward where through the window two bleary-eyed dogs, half wagging their tails, sat up in their baskets wondering what to do. I wondered what to do. Now how could I make a racket and wake everyone up? I mean, you couldn't do such a thing, could you?

I crept back to the shed, but planning my onslaught for the morning.

'I don't mind being down the bottom of the garden in "The Shed". I'm used to it. I know I'm a:

neurotic

irrational

obsessional

illogical

eccentric with a problem getting to sleep when there's noise but:

I CAN'T HELP IT.

I asked twice for a key. Never mind that the latest equipment in "The Shed" didn't seem to need it - I needed it! Aren't human beings more important than all that convoluted technological know-how? So why wouldn't anyone take the trouble to find me the f***ing key?'

Alright, swearing is off-limits and I noticed one grandchild in the kitchen, jaw-dropped-wide.

Then her meek little voice chimed up, 'I knew where the key was kept.' We all suddenly switched and stared at this still small voice of calm, the pause button on hold.

…'I'd have given it to you, grandma.'

A silence ensued and I couldn't puke any more of the speech fermentation I'd planned. I just embraced this little one in a bear-hug of joy. Then all attention switched to the lop-eared rabbit fitfully thumping his feet on the floor of the cage, his ears dangling over the precipitous void.

.…'Coffee, anyone?' someone said.

\* \* \*

# A LETTER TO VITA

15th June 1954

Dear Vita,

Just a note to let you know I'm in Clover! …and our morning wake-up call could as well be tolling bells 'cause it's Tuesday, 'Number Nines' day. I've a surprise for you…wait for it… I'm now a nurse! And to use the nursing lingo, 'number nines' are laxatives (so called when part of soldiers' kit in the Second World War) renowned for their 'purgative qualities'.  They're what the night staff give out here on a Monday night when they come on duty, and put the patients on bed-pans before they go off at six next morning. Then it's our turn!  Are you interested in a job?!

I must explain the patients here are mostly paralysed and need something really strong like that to make them 'go'. So after we've, like, got them sorted (there are four or five to a room) and sanitized the sluices (there are two on each corridor) and scrubbed up, you'll guess not many of us can face breakfast after that!

'Who's on Lady bloody Clover wing?' - that's how Nurse Rolfe greeted me at the top of the stairs. She's avoiding the lift - got stuck in it for an hour going off-duty last week and is still raging! We call her 'Nurse Wolf' 'cause she bares her teeth (you can see they're false) and crunches you up with some of the language she comes out with and she *always* shouts.

'Oh good, it's Sheila,' she yelled this morning, and a sort-of-smile kind-of lurked then clamped onto her face. It wasn't just ordinary friendly, it had a hidden agenda. I mean, I'm popular because I'm young and fit and do more than my fair share when we're lifting the patients, but Wolf and most of the nurses aren't and pretend they're lifting when they're not. They've worked it down to a fine art and don't miss a trick. You can't really blame them, they probably feel their own arthritic problems aren't too far behind the patients' (we're overdue here for hoists and chairlifts by the way).

Remember I was looking for a job to get through college? Well I found this one advertised at a 'Home and Hospital for Gentlewomen'. I think the powers that be haven't decided yet if it's one or the other so they've hedged their bets and called it both. On the board outside what it *actually* says is 'Home and Hospital for Incurables'. Can you believe that, Vita? Can you imagine anything more insensitive for a patient to see than that? But, no contest, it's run like a hospital - we all wear these uniforms and there's a sister on each floor with an S.R.N.

If, by any chance, you happened to miss that awful sign, which is unlikely, and came through the portico into the hall - polished oak floor, brass plates on the wall with CMG or Bart. or something-or-other after the names, you'd think you'd walked into an exclusive men's club. Everything that's brass is polished up to the nines, down to the door-knobs and hinges. There's a Victorian table (polished mahogany) in the middle with a flower-arrangement and a visitors' book - that's polished too - no kidding - it's leather!

When you get up here to Lady Clover Wing, there's a corridor with a lino floor and a row of wheelchairs down one side. You tick the patients' names 'in' or 'out' on the door of each ward but they're rarely out - once in a blue moon. We take them as far as the day-room and that's it. Occasionally relatives or suchlike call with some lilies or 'Fry's Turkish Delight' to share round, but not often. It's so boring. If only they'd try to take some of them out to trendy, lively shopping arcades or something. I bet Lady Clover, whoever she is, never comes up here. Hey, maybe she brings each patient a pair of bed-socks at Christmas!

Oh Vita, yesterday was one to chalk up. Sister called us all into her office.

'We're taking the patients down to the garden after their elevenses, Staff,' (they've normally had their elevenses by ten). 'The gardeners have just mown the lawn and it's such a warm and sunny day, don't you think?'

We were thinking it'd be tricky (though Nurse Wolf wouldn't put it quite like that) and it was. *This* lady wanted her handbag and a headscarf with her teeth wrapped up in it, *that* lady wanted all her money put in her pockets, but Sister Knowles isn't one to just give orders. Actually, she reminds me of your mum with her boundless energy - rolls up her sleeves and heaves and squeezes the wheelchairs in and out of the lifts with the rest of us.

Anyway, by the time we got the last patient down to the newly mown lawn, the first was too hot or needed 'to go' and wanted to come back up. In short, we all ended up exhausted.

You get a real shock to see how physically handicapped the patients really are when they come here (they don't cater for the mentally afflicted, by the way). But they're so stoical with their conditions it's… how can I say? It's just… awesome. Honestly, it makes me feel ashamed to be fit and well. I'll tell you about Miss Spire, for instance. She's got a specially made wooden bed with wheels like a pram. She doesn't sit up much so there's a curved mirror above it which lets her see what's going on in the ward, and the picture of the fiancé she was going to marry. Trouble is when she got MS it was broken off.

'Fetch my trunk out when you're free, Nurse, I'll show you my bridal dress and veil; they've never been worn,' she said one day last week. They all have a trunk in the depot for their stuff, their keepsakes and that. Nice, isn't it? The porters are none too pleased when they've got to bring them up, but Barry's always willing. The staff said his mother was in here once and the cost of it has left him skint.

Anyway, he brought up the trunk and even propped the back wheels of her bed up on wooden blocks so she could see.

'Oh, it would be a treat to see you in it, Sheila. Do you think you could put it on?' she said. 'You're about the same size as me when I was your age.'

Honestly, it knocked me out, Vita!

'Oh Miss Spire, I couldn't - honest I couldn't!' I said.

'Not for my sake?'

Could *you* refuse? I put on the dress, but I couldn't face the veil, and posed and walked about for her. She watched intently and her eyes gleamed and she seemed to hold her breath and I got worried then because they got all watery. I wondered if she was seeing herself going to the altar all those years ago? Anyway I hugged her and my eyes welled up a bit too. Then we put on our smiles and I wiped her face and we started to laugh.

She was so grateful, I was upset.

'However you're placed there's someone worse,' she said. Her frail body, her inner strength - it's so humbling, you know? They're all like that in their own way and I felt kind of numb as I wrapped the dress in its tissue paper.

So that's Miss Spire. I could tell you about poor Miss Hood who happened to... No, I'd better, not you'd only be upset, and - hey ho! That's my break over, so I'll have to finish now, Vita.

I must admit I'm glad when we get near the end of a shift there's only the lifting to face, the rest is chatting the patients up and settling them down. It's tough - you don't realise the half of it - but I just feel it's more than a job. With these poorly people who tend to be forgotten, I like to think you can make a difference, you know? Even on Tuesdays.

Love to everyone.
As ever, Sheila.

\* \* \*

# AFTER THE TEN O'CLOCK NEWS

It was Alex's habit to take his book to the toilet after the ten o'clock news each night - a ritual, you could say - and I'd already have gone up to bed.

One morning, he said, 'For the past few nights I've noticed a huge black spider come out of the plug-hole in the shower-tray. I'm amazed a spider of such dimensions can get through one spoke of a wheel-shaped hole only five centimeters diameter in total. It must live down the pipe and only come up at night.'

'How can it? As soon as you shower it'll drown and be washed away.'

'As a matter of fact, I haven't showered since I saw it, and you always shower upstairs, so he's kind of - settled in - I suppose. It's his size that unsettles me.'

'Where does it go?'

'Not far, he moves very slowly as if he's not well, but when I touched him up with the lavatory brush two nights ago, he scuttled off through the door at a terrific rate into the utility room. I thought that'd be the end of him but last night he appeared up through the hole again, slow, as before. I've looked up 'large spiders' on the internet and the one that fitted his description most was the Black House Spider. It read "Poisonous but not lethal…certain people bitten by one experience severe pain around the bite-site", and other things, and that it is commonly found in gutters and toilets. So that seems to fit, doesn't it?'

'Well the remedy is quite simple: turn the shower-head to very hot and leave it on full power for ten minutes. That'll get rid of it.'

I was asleep before Alex came up to bed. The next morning I said I hadn't heard the shower the previous night. He said he didn't put it on; the Black House Spider had beaten him to it and was already ensconced in the middle of the shower-tray.

'I've called him Groucho Marx.'

'Why?'

'Well, Groucho had a night-shirt and night-cap and a thick black moustache and he was moody and…it seemed to fit, somehow. Anyway, I couldn't flush him down the hole.'

'Well he's - it's - not there now. I've had a good look.'

'No, he only comes out after the ten o'clock news. Thing is, it's not easy to get off the toilet in case he does a runner out of the shower-tray. I emptied the cistern a few times but that didn't worry him, but - he's big, you know? And poisonous. I finished reading *Gone with the Wind* last night but then started Chapter One again, keeping an eye on Groucho, just in case.'

'Just in case what?'

'Oh I don't know - I just didn't want to get bitten. I passed the time recalling some Groucho quotes: "Either he's dead or my watch has stopped" - except my watch is still going and he's definitely not dead! D'you know the one - "I've had a perfectly wonderful evening, but this wasn't it"? Kind of apt don't you think?'

'Alex, I'm getting rather worried about you, and if you can't use the downstairs shower, use the upstairs one for a while.'

'No, I won't do that, you might be asleep.'

'Then I'll come down and flush it away. Alright?'

'No, don't do that. I'll touch him up with the lavatory brush again. He may scamper off into the utility room like before. Plus, I'll find a good read to distract me. Umm…what about Kafka's *Metamorphosis*? - except it's no joke, I'll tell him.'

This morning I woke up to find Alex sitting in front of the dressing-table mirror. I asked him if he'd got rid of that arachnid.

'You were a long time, I nearly came down.' Then I saw him in the mirror. 'Aah! Alex, what have you done to your face?'

'I've had a bad night, Freda. I waited till eleven o'clock this time, but Groucho was still there when I went in. I'd shut the shower door, but there he was in the middle of the tray looking at me through the glass, none too pleased.

I told him I wasn't going to open the door in case he rushed at me, but I wondered what he'd find to eat in there, so I inched it ajar and he moved slowly forwards and squatted on the rim. I thought if I suddenly shut the sliding-door I could slice him in half, but he guessed what I was thinking and shot straight out between my feet. I jumped up and my trousers and underpants dropped down on top of him.

I was distraught. I prised my feet out of them and made for the utility room but I'd forgotten I'd closed the door and barged straight into it! I've flattened my nose and I got a hell of a nose-bleed, I can tell you. Without thinking I grabbed my trousers to find a handkerchief and there was Groucho, his eight legs curled under him, looking quite bemused.

'Enough is enough,' I said. "I never forget a face but, in your case, I'll be glad to make an exception".  He seemed to take the hint and crawled through a pool of my nose-bleed into the utility room. Frankly, I didn't like seeing his red dripping hairy legs, so I splashed some water over him to clean him up and opened the back door. "This is the best way out for both of us," I said, showing him the door. He sidled out on to the step, swiveled round, then lifted up two wet legs in a military salute and disappeared into the night.

I couldn't move, staring at Alex.  He was sweating. He said he had muscle pains and a headache and his foot had swelled up.

'You've been bitten, Alex, and you're hallucinating. I'm going to call an ambulance. Darling, are you listening to me? Alex…don't you recognise me? Your wife, Alex?'

He just waved *Gone with the Wind* at me and said, '"Outside of a dog, a book is a man's best friend; inside of a dog it's too dark to read."'

* * *

# THE QUESTIONNAIRE

The face of the other is the primary site of moral obligation.

Emmanual Levinas

A reply from the Housing Department finally arrived. It was in the form of a questionnaire.

### _How long have you occupied your flat?_

'I seem to have been here years and years,' she sighed, and noticed the words: _rehoused due to post-traumatic stress._

'They haven't even bothered to remove the client confidentiality addendum, typical or what?'

_Since January,_ she wrote in the space provided.

'It was snowing and I've got Renaud's syndrome and I couldn't even bring the cat for company. NO PETS ALLOWED.'

## *When did you first contact the Maintenance Department about your boiler?*

She scribbled cursorily *when it didn't work,* then making an effort to control her irritation, crossed it out.

'Umm...after January, so it must have been February - no - March, the crocuses were out. There's something in them the birds must like 'cause they pulled all the petals off.' She wrote *March* then read *PLEASE INCLUDE ALL BOILER INSTRUCTIONS WHEN YOU REPLY TO THIS QUESTIONNAIRE.*

'I wonder why the man...girl upstairs doesn't take the milk in. There are now three bottles on the step. She'll need to get the housing department to repair the window; the boys from number 16 throw stones at it. There's a hole, and cracks in the glass, it'll be draughty.

"Include all boiler instructions"? That doesn't make sense! Why send all instructions to the Maintenance Section when the man'll need them here to mend it? I bet once they get in someone's in-tray they'll never make the out-tray. Perhaps that's the idea - a dodgy-ditch-it or lost-in-transit end to what-a-pain-job.

That sums me up really - lost in transit - from Tomás to Dick and from Dick to... No, Gerry was one step too far. I saw what he was capable of. I knew what he was going to do. When I was posted into his orbit - him high on the liquor, high on the glories of the past, I realised "the terrible beauty" of Connolly and Pearse he talked about had been seared by a brutality that was anything but glorious. He knew it himself. In a kind of desperation he'd quote Yeats – "Too long a sacrifice/can make a stone of the heart".'

She gazed through the window at humps of dead grass bulging through the boggy garden patch. 'All I can see is a landscape of waste ... I can't go on! Wherever I end up... I can't go on!'

She had been advised by the 'Special Unit' it was not helpful to dwell on the past. They said she must move on but she knew, wherever they re-housed her, whatever identity they gave her, she'd always be 'other'.

## *Are you in a position to pay for repairs?*

'Jesus no, all that's happened can't be repaired. He saw me twitching the curtain, his eyes burned 'informer' indelibly into me as they wrenched his hand from the door-handle and bludgeoned him away. Mother of God, how can that ever be repaired?' She stared into the void.

'It's history, they said. What's left is...' she looked at her new name written on the questionnaire - *Geraldine Foxall*. 'Yes, I do love foxes ... they're hounded too till ... the end, or the hunters cry "gone to earth".'

Bitterly she scrawled *Yes, I have money for the necessities of life.*

She watched the man-turned-girl on the doorstep rummaging for her key to the upstairs flat and taking in one bottle of milk.

'My guess is she's been rehoused here too. She's very tall and - angular. Her legs look thin, she'd be better wearing jeans, but I suppose she wouldn't like that. She's worked hard on her hair - bouffant style... Hmm, a bit too precise, a bit like the wig I wore to cover my shaved head. Her make-up is rather thick - maybe her skin needs it.'

She'd come across Zoë - that's what they called her - the previous day in a charity shop, helping out. Her voice was the difficulty, deep on the downward inflections. Her face seemed to jerk into a smile when she chatted with the customers and when they left it closed down, her mouth locked-tight.

'She's had it rough - we're two of a kind really - have issues with identity. Those kids from number 16 know she's a 'he', that's why they throw stones at her window.'

She bought a pair of jeans while in the shop and noticed, as Zoë counted out the change, her long fingers displayed numerous sparkling rings, her nails were painted star-dust pink and her large hands jingled with rainbow bangles on her wrist. It looked as if her gender was an exclamation marked by her glitter and bling. She thought perhaps it would be better not to overdo it.

Thud! Thump! 'What's that?'

She threw open the window and looked up. Bottles of milk had gashed the window upstairs, the milk spurting out and spilling down into runnels along the sill. She rushed to the door to see the backs of four youths laughing up the street. Her instinct was to go after them, to take them on with her bare hands, with brute muscle, with gritted teeth, fists clenched to knuckles sharp - but as her blood surged, officialdom intervened, had re-branded her 'Geraldine Foxall' and she'd agreed to follow their instructions.

It was not what she'd expected, having to follow instructions in return for her security. She wanted…she wanted to look into the face of Zoë, and acknowledge her obligation to someone other than herself but her hands were tied. Her fingers froze on the door-handle as she murmured 'gone to earth.'

## *Are you in a position to be available during the day?*

'I have no 'position'. I exist. I have a new name and a safe-house - the ground-floor flat.'

*Yes, I'm available during the day,* she wrote.

* * *

# THE THEATRE TRIP

'You've got the boys' tickets, Dave, and it's curtain up any moment.'

'No curtains, Vanessa - the Swan is a forward-thrust stage,' he joked.

She grimaced at his one-upmanship in front of the students. 'Peter's got them, actually, and he's parking the bus.'

'He'd better hurry up, they won't let us in after the houselights have gone down.'

There were mutterings of disappointment that the boarded stage seemed pretty bare - you could certainly see the wood for the trees! But the girls knuckled down and were soon sketching the ground-plan and set. She hoped they'd refuse to supply their endeavours to the boys, who were already crackling the wrappings off sweets, and prayed they wouldn't be exploding their bags of popcorn as well!

The cast were uniformly superb and Adrian Noble had delivered a fine production of *The Cherry Orchard*. She needn't have worried that the girls would find it an anti-climax. After all, they'd come a hundred and fifty miles to see this subtle tragic and comic story of gentry facing ruin. Tsarist Russia was coming to an end (symbolised by the felling of their beloved cherry orchard), and the family was struggling, in vain, to recognise or come to terms with the approaching revolution. Yes, the Swan interpretation was spot-on, she decided.

The students were studying Chekhov for their A-levels, and this RSC performance had proved a real educational boost for them. Vanessa was very upbeat as they all piled into the minibus.

There was so much to discuss but engaging in any meaningful conversation at eleven o'clock at night was not feasible for these young minds. They just plugged in their Walkmans or chatted about eighteenth birthday bashes at their local discos or who was causing a stir with whom, till, their energy spent, a lull set in.

At the back of the bus, Dave was sitting with his group of 'in' boys who remained animated, exchanging jokes of a dubious nature, the most dubious seemingly supplied by him. His broad Glaswegian dialect could be heard above the rest. She was slightly uncomfortable about Dave. He was new to the English department of the boys' school and gossip had it that he was 'pretty chummy' with the select few he invited to his pad. He certainly didn't seem at all interested in the girls!

Vanessa was beginning to doze off when the minibus lost power and Peter pulled over to the hard shoulder. After he and Dave had conferred, they came over to tell her they'd run out of petrol. She was mortified! How could they be so incompetent? Here they were, on the busiest stretch of the M6 at half past eleven at night with lorries flashing their lights and sounding their horns as they shot past them lodged on the hard shoulder. Then, unbelievably, Peter told them to get out and push the bus towards the bank.

'I'm not having the girls doing that,' she exclaimed. 'In fact, they've all got to go and sit on top of the bank out of harm's way.' There were no arguments, the girls were glad enough to scramble up the bank and started sharing around their mobiles to update their parents, no doubt making the most of the high drama.

Dave, Peter and the boys proceeded with their dangerous manoeuvre, the passing traffic hooting at their folly, but it was accomplished. The boys proudly dusted-off in front of the bus while the girls above huddled together in the cold night wind.

Janice came down to the bottom of the bank. 'I haven't got any insulin and I should have taken it an hour ago.'

'I didn't know you were diabetic?' Vanessa felt she knew the girls well, so this came as a complete surprise.

'I don't tell people, they don't need to know.'

But now there *was* a pressing need.

'Umm…would you like me to ask if anyone has any sweets?'

'No, that won't do any good.'

'How do you feel?'

'Alright now, but how long will it be before I get home?'

'I don't know, Janice, but it shouldn't be long'.

Vanessa went down to the men, told them the problem, and watched their faces drop.

'One of the girls is ill,' Peter shouted to the boys. 'Has anyone got any ideas about how we can speed things up, chaps?'

They all looked towards the huddle of girls where Janice's face flushed up and she aimed a consummate traitor-glare at Vanessa, who guessed that by now the whole predicament was being relayed to their parents.

'My granddad lives this side of Birmingham. I can ring and ask if he can bring a can of petrol, sir.'

'Try it,' said Peter. It worked. The boy's grandfather arranged to come on at exit eleven north of Birmingham, so Vanessa felt some sense of relief. It was short-lived. Peter's insensitive yelling to the boys on the hard shoulder started the girls quizzing Janice about what was wrong with her, while the boys were muttering, elbowing and winking at each other about 'girls' problems'. Janice looked drained and likely to burst into tears any minute. Not wanting her to lose face, Vanessa beckoned her over and rummaging in her shoulder-bag, very obviously produced some tablets and whispered 'I know you don't want these 'Settlers' but you could pretend I've given you them for your stomach, couldn't you?' Janice nodded and went back to the girls, simulating a chewing action, and they seemed to accept this explanation.

Both grandfather and the AA arrived within minutes of each other, so more than enough petrol was obtained to get them home.

* *

The following day two of the girls seized the opportunity to come in late to school, not having arrived home till the early hours. Three more parents phoned the headmistress to complain, not unreasonably, about their previous night's concerns and Vanessa was summoned to the high altar to explain herself.

There were no seats in front of the headmistress's desk so she stood to face the recriminations. It was thoroughly reprehensible to make such foolhardy arrangements for a theatre visit with the boys' school next door. (She never encouraged fraternisation with *that school*; the rivalry between them had long been ugly and intense, hence the obstacles Vanessa always encountered when casting parts for the boys.) The dressing-down continued. She had been seriously remiss in not taking information on the girl's medical condition from the staff notice-board. Her riposte, that Janice Carter's condition didn't appear on the board because her parents had chosen not to disclose it, emboldened her to add that for any further school trips to productions, students would have to make their own arrangements to theatre venues.

It clearly rankled, and the headmistress produced a folder from the filing-cabinet.

'Details of your employment here require you to accompany pupils on all educational visits outside of school.' She lowered the folder and her bullet-eyes took aim over her half-glasses. 'And I strongly resent the tone of your remarks, Miss Binney.'

Vanessa held the look, didn't blink and thought 'shall I take her on?' She seemed taller than usual, her black hair tightly set round her face. Oddly, it was her feet that made the strongest impression - long, with pointed shoes turned outwards when she walked. As her body depended heavily on them, she never failed to sound the alert with those thuds. The Black Watch tartan suit she always seemed to wear suggested a Calvinistic chill, which made Vanessa suddenly throw caution to the wind.

'*I* resent being admonished for performing a play, any play, by Brecht and being forbidden to stage *Oh, What a Lovely War.* I resent having to clear all the equipment from the studio at an hour's notice to accommodate a governors' lunch *and* being reprimanded for leaving the masks of Greek gods hanging on the wall.' There was no going back. 'In fact, I wish to tender my resignation.'

They glowered at each other, then, to Vanessa's amazement, the woman seemed to back off.

'This is a rather hasty decision. I suggest you come and see me tomorrow when you've really had time to think. There's the bell, and I have a lesson to attend - and will you add

Janice Carter's name to the medical list in the staff room.'

With that, she strode out of the room.

'I've actually won that round,' Vanessa gulped. She swallowed. 'Who knows, there may even be room for manoeuvre on Burnham Scale One! ... But, do I really want this job?'

\* \* \*

# REHEARSING *THE CHERRY ORCHARD*

'…Yes, of course. Anya must wear white. She of all the characters - pure young innocent, driven back to the past, and such an unusually late May frost.'

'But she says in Act One: "I didn't sleep all the four nights of our journey…and now I feel so chilly."'

'You would wear it in Act Two - the edge of the cherry orchard, late afternoon, when she says that today is marvellous here, you know? - and Trofimov says that the weather is wonderful and sees the whole of Russia as their orchard? … Umm… I have a white dress which might fit you. It could just have the right 'look' for Anya. Anyway, I'll bring it in and you can try it… The Art Department is doing a great job with the set; they're putting frost-bitten buds amongst the blossoms. You'll look lovely in white, Rebecca.'

I put out the lights, rang the caretaker and collected the odds-and-bobs. They always leave stuff... It is important for them to discover the sub-text for themselves rather than have it pointed out. I like to watch it gradually dawning on them, now they've started moving the script.

I found my wedding-dress in a suitcase behind the wardrobe with other redundant clothes. It's of coarse cotton lace and the matt finish is good for picking up mood-lighting. What a small waist! It wouldn't fit me now. Oh, those plastic underwear buttons my neighbour got for the wrists! I'd thought they'd be little pearl-droplets. Actually they'll stand out better from a distance than the delicate cuffs I'd hoped for. She only charged £6 so what did I expect?

I remember thinking maybe I could dye it, and make a dance outfit or something with the lace afterwards. The whole thing was 'run up' one week-end and I was married the following Saturday morning! If I give it a shake - or maybe it'll get ironed before the next rehearsal.

* *

'OK Anya. Take it from line 41.'

*My room, my windows, just as if I had never been away. I am home! Tomorrow morning I shall get up, and run straight into the orchard. Oh, if only I could sleep. I didn't sleep all through the journey. I was so worried and anxious.*

I didn't sleep the night before the wedding. The flat was too crowded - my mother, my brother, my very-pregnant sister-in-law. It didn't go down well that I'd become a Catholic. They asked what was the point of half the ceremony in Latin. Mum had had a fall recently and wasn't really well. They complained they couldn't keep standing up and kneeling down. I said it didn't matter, they could sit.

*...everyone is fond of you, everyone respects you ... but Uncle dear, you should keep silent, just keep silent. What were you saying just now about my mother, your sister? What did you say it for?*

'Anya, it's coming alive now, you're expressing more confidently what you feel.'

I remember going to the church the night before the wedding in my brother's car with an armful of flowers to put somewhere round the altar.

'I can't go through with it!' I cried.

Becky likes the dress. She moves so well and is quite unaware of it - she's a natural... It was raining the next day, but my brother said I looked like the fairy on the Christmas tree in that dress. It was quite something coming from him. He's not one for paying compliments, but I guess he had to say something - he was giving me away after all... Oh, the white Rolls-Royce! All dolled-up in flowers and ribbons as if the car was the bride driving up to take the marriage vows!

'Prompter, can you read in Trofimov please?'

*Forward! We are progressing irresistibly towards the bright star that glows in the distance! Forward! Don't lag behind, friends.*

'Thanks. He's got a rugby away-match on tonight. Anya? Don't worry! He'll have his lines next week - your instinct is right, Becky - it's enough to "be". Remember Chekhov's words "they act too much"?'

'It is enough to "be"', I said to myself as I stood holding a bouquet of apricot roses at the church door. 'There are the people, and there he is! Standing before the altar, waiting for me.'

I've often thought since, how awful it must be if a bride, standing like that, at the last minute thinks she might have made a mistake and shouldn't be standing there at all. I did not doubt for a second that this was what I really,

really wanted. Happiness, yes, it beckons as the organ reaches its top note, all the stops pulled out, beckons as the pipes reverberate down the aisle.

* *

> *Forward! We are progressing irresistibly towards the bright star that glows in the distance! Forward! Friends.*

Good. Trofimov *has* learnt his lines and there's a bit of panache about him tonight. Anya's transformed him and the dress looks well - or, rather - she's owning it tonight.

> *Look! The moon is rising.*
> *Yes, Anya, the moon is rising. Happiness, it is here. It is coming nearer and nearer. I already hear its foot-steps.*

* *

'What'll I do with the dress?'

'Oh, it's done its job; it can go in the costume-cupboard with the rest of the stuff. You've recovered, Becky? After all the accolades?'

'Yes. It's funny how clothes can change your perceptions of everything. It kind of lingers - you know? Anya's wrench from the past to face her new life. And the audience watching you is somehow...like wearing the dress...as if you're wearing new things. And with all the people watching, you're different.'

'I know.'

\* \* \*

Translation of *The Cherry Orchard* by Elisaveta Fen 1959. (Penguin 1986)

# THE LIE

I'll begin by letting you know I've never been over the moon about holidays. They don't grab me as they do most people. Don't get me wrong, a hard-earned rest in some out-of-the-way place wouldn't go amiss, but a holiday? No. Really, the idea never struck me enough to make the effort - not like challenges. I absolutely do challenges; they've marked me out, you could say, and I'm always up for the tough call. It all started, as far as I can understand it, with a lie. I'll tell you how it was.

I wanted to write, or, more accurately, to *be* a writer, and after slugging it out for a year in the secretarial sixth form, I got a job on *The Country Gentlemen's Association* magazine. My initiation, my 'launch into print', was a book review: *Lovely Peggy, The Life and Times of Margaret Woffington* (the theatre being my other passion). But I'd taken so long to get the thing down, I figured I'd never make it in journalism.

The next challenge was to make it as an actor, but with every part I played I got stage-fright. I kept getting more and more petrified I'd 'corpse', and after I did I was plagued with chronic diarrhea, so that was that.

One good thing came out of it - challenge number three - I found I could teach, especially directing and producing stuff, where there was never any shortage of challenges. True, they brought struggle, heartache and the rest, but sometimes a feeling of 'getting there' which brought satisfaction and just occasionally amazement, which made me stick at it till - eureka! That spangled moment when I'd be blown away. And when I do…get to that magic place… I can't describe it - except it's like when I saw Orson Welles play Othello or Patrick McGoohan play Brand (Ibsen). Just awesome is all I can say and I still do stick at it, working for that moment; it's like a drug. But, same as anyone else, you've got to come down from the high-octane stuff sometimes and take a break, and for me it's only breaks - just a breather, you understand. Definitely not holidays.

Anyway, enough of that… Except, as I said, I can pinpoint the exact time it all started. Quite frankly, it's not hard to recall.

*'Hi Margaret, it's busy today.'*
*'I'll say. You hold the seats and I'll order the usual.'*
*'OK.'*
*'Two sugars?'*
*'Please'.*

I'll never forget how unhappy I was on that day. She was my classmate - Margaret. She played Cecily and I played Gwendolen in the school play, for heaven's sake. We both faced the daily grind to London and the same menial typing jobs, except she could do shorthand and mine was zero. Anyway, to escape from the tyranny of it all we'd been saving for a holiday in Venice - you know, the one of a lifetime?  For months we hardly talked about anything else when we met on a lunch-break once a week.

Then one week I'd gone for an audition to this drama school. Treble surprise - I was accepted. The problem was money - what problem isn't? But I knew that the next week I was going to ditch our planned holiday. Call it shameful, cowardly, dastardly, despicable - go on with the list of expletives, why don't you?

*'Margaret, I've got some bad news.'*
*'Here's your sandwich. We're lucky, the last two tuna-and-sweetcorn. Yes? What?'*

*'Umm…my mum's sick and…and my dad's done a runner…and she hasn't any money… I've got to help out so… I can't go to Venice.'*

As always seems to happen at a critical moment, she was just starting to drink her coffee. She swallowed hard and stared at me. I looked down at the sandwich. I can't tell you how I felt except it was betrayal and humiliation - the hell of all the lies - just all of it.

The boy who played Dr. Chasuble in the school play (it was *The Importance of Being Earnest)* was kind-of my boyfriend at the time - mainly because he was kind. Nicknamed 'Spratt' he was gangly and awkward, all elbows and double-joints. The point is, he was a friend of Margaret's family.

I'm telling you all this because months after the event, I bumped into him - he was at ICL - just behind the Albert Hall where I was doing the drama. It's no great surprise he was very standoffish. He said he'd been 'nonplussed' at what I had done. He waited awhile for me to say something … He waited …

'Why couldn't you tell her the truth?  She'd have understood.'

'I don't know  -  I was too mean, embarrassed.'

'She was so upset and let down that you could lie like that. I couldn't make excuses for what you did.… I didn't want to.'

'I know, I'm sorry, I'm not worth it.'

He waited again … I felt so alone.

'Her mother died at Christmas.'

'Oh.'

We just looked at each other and I walked away.

I stared at the Albert Hall where I'd been so eager to go. It'll never have been worth it, I thought.

All these 'challenges' I've taken on were to make it right. And all the holidays I've turned my back on were to try and get rid of the cursed albatross round my neck. Is it the truth I'm telling - or is it a lie? I really want to know. Tell me.

\* \* \*

# THE CHRISTENING

'Well, that's Dilly christened, and not before time at twenty-one months old! Oh, I'd so hoped mother's beautiful christening-gown (she's dead now, R.I.P.) would have come in for at least one grandchild, and after three boys, Dilys provided the ideal opportunity - but no. The sacrament of baptism has taken place now she's finished being a baby and started being a toddler, so that idea went out with the bathwater, so to speak.

George, I've concluded the occasion all started to go wrong because we changed for church too early. Dilly sported a new flowery dress, that's neither here nor there, but nobody had thought about any lunch. The children would have been so much more amenable if they'd had something in their stomachs, don't you agree?'

'Er… Yes, of course.'

'And, of course, mistake number two - we arrived fifteen minutes early.'

'We did. We certainly did.'

'Unfortunately so did Gary, the boys' favourite uncle, and, as usual, he dazzled them with the prospect of playing games of football which they imagined would last forever. I think that's what set them off tearing round the church aisles where Father Buckley was making preparations for the baptism. Don't *you* think so?'

'Yes, absolutely.'

'A sense of foreboding had already crept into my mind as I watched you get them to the back of the porch, until parents of school friends arrived with *their* offspring. You know it was so wrong of them letting their children band together and troop off to the pews nearest the font, as from that vantage point we were powerless to prevent an oncoming tide of catastrophes.

One boy, clearly not having been taught how to behave in the house of God, produced a pack of cards! That's what attracted the attention of our pumped-up grandsons in the front pew, and they all ended up facing the wrong way. Luckily I managed to spirit the cards into my pocket and quell the surge of noisy resentment which echoed round the church, but what I can't understand is why the owners of that unruly bunch didn't intervene instead of hiding their amusement at *me* doing the hushing and shushing. I thought it was very uncharitable of them, George.'

'Yes it was, and you handled it very… robustly I must say.'

'Of course, Jessica and our son-in-law weren't able to help as they were too pre-occupied trying to restrain Dilly at the font. She was getting more and more alarmed at the proceedings and started howling almost like a wolf! It quite drowned poor Father Buckley's efforts to deliver his introductory homily, so eventually he had to abandon that part of the ceremony… George, would you feel more comfortable if you changed out of your glad rags? They make you look rather stiff.'

'What a good idea - I'll just go and do that.'

'Jessica is lovely, naturally, but she is a bit scatterbrained. I remember the time she had an interview in London and asked us to collect her stuff from her student digs. Oh, the mess! It was unbelievable! Rats had obviously got at my 'Christy' towels which lay in a soggy heap on the bathroom floor. Cousin Mary (she's a nun, of course) said we should leave everything and go, but I had to salvage some things - the photographs - and what *did* irritate was all the money scattered about - loose change she'd call it - but it added up! Yes, now you can relax dear, you always look best in your cords.

I must say you had placed yourself very strategically behind the pillar at the end of the pew, but then my heart started to sink as I watched you creep out stalking our youngest grandson. He had taken it into his head to investigate the jug of holy water and the cloth and candle on the side-table, just as the priest was approaching for the next phase of the proceedings. I held my breath - the whole congregation held its breath, but you performed a miracle darling, an absolute miracle, in retrieving them in the nick of time, just as Father finished his text and reached for the cloth and jug to wet Dilly's head. I noticed his hands were starting to tremble and he spilt the holy water.

By now Dilly was almost in convulsions being held over the font by our increasingly apprehensive daughter and son-in-law. Her sponsor was even more alarmed, and an ex-professional rugby player, no less! I really don't think any of the congregation heard a word of the baptismal rites being bestowed upon our fractious granddaughter, which was, after all, the essence of the sacrament.

It was when Father ascended the pulpit, in some haste, to wind up the ceremony that all eyes became transfixed upon our other two grandsons, who climbed up some steps behind him and, would you believe, started to re-arrange The Holy Family below! He didn't look down - I think he was pretending he didn't see them. Dear God! Yet again, you, my shining knight, came to the rescue, reinstated the statuettes and bundled the boys, none too gently this time I'm glad to say, back into our pew.'

'Well someone had to do it.'

'Never mind, here we are, home at last and quite exhausted. It's funny, when I asked you why the children had behaved so badly, do you remember what you said?'

'No, I don't think I remember anything very much.'

'You said it was because they needed filling with stuffed potatoes! But it was because Dilly was the wrong age. If she had been a little baby, she wouldn't have felt much different from having her head doused with water in church or at home. Then if she had been three years old, say, she could have understood at least a little of what was going on, but, at twenty-one months, the whole performance must have been frightful.

As regards the boys, they know what happens at Mass; they go, on the whole, every week. But when their friends and long-absent relatives arrive all dressed up, bringing presents for Dilly, I suppose they could be forgiven for regarding it as a kind of party, don't you? George? …George?'

Oh, I expect he's popped off to the *Nag's Head*. He likes his Bushmill's malt when he's had a stressful day. Oh, he's been a real brick. I don't know what we'd do without him. I think… *I* need something to eat, I'm feeling rather queasy.

Parents these days don't help. They don't bother so much about manners and religious observances as they used to. Yes, queasy. Things will be better at Christmas when a grandson will be properly rehearsed for his role as an altar server.

It's strange, really strange, now I look back on it all, I can't help asking myself whether it… matters. It has to be done properly…properly. I *do* feel very odd. Otherwise it gets all… muddled up and no-one will know if it actually means…if it actually means what it is supposed to…mean. The dressing up, the kneeling down, splashing the w-a-t-e-r…it's beginning to dis-ap-pear into - the - distance… Like dis-ap- pear into… Like…the end of a film, when everything becomes…small-er and vag-uer and fain-ter… Till there's…nothing left but… a… mist.

\* \* \*

# THE BROTHERS

They were as different as 'de chalk from de goats' milk, de moment dey came into de light,' as Bella put it when the boys were born - and 'a year to de week between each odda. Is'n dat surprisin?'

By 1980 the young boys had been summarily dispatched by their father from Southern Rhodesia to motherland Britain, which had at that time been similarly dispatched from its African colony. Their father, however, remained 'incommunicado' in Salisbury.

Bella, their nanny, had been right. The brothers were opposites in nature and, now in the homeland, were nurtured at the butt-end of a failed marriage, a chaotic motherhood and a struggling grandmotherhood, which was more than enough to hamper anyone's life chances. So it was not surprising that the clash of belonging and exclusion, perplexity and teenage angst stoked up in them an indeterminate sense of who they were.

But Anatole grew up identifying himself wholeheartedly with nature in all its diversity. He was vegetarian, but quietly. Working for Oxfam (living only a few minutes by bicycle from its headquarters in the Banbury Road) he found himself often in the eye of its administrative storms in his endeavours to aid the hungry and oppressed. His other eye focused on 'SPEAK', the animal rights campaign group, and rumours of university plans for a new animal research laboratory greatly disturbed him.

Rafe, the younger-brother-by-a-year, identified himself wholeheartedly with human-kind and flourished in Oxford's other city landscape of arcades, Indian takeaways, Burger King and 'McWorld's' values of consumerism.

The boys bedded down happily in Driffield College where their mother and the Head of College Maintenance were 'an item'. It enabled them all to occupy a suite of rooms in the east wing, which overlooked a rather beautiful quad.

Driffield was one of Oxford's smaller seats of learning. Scouts had little to do but take messages, and people came and went without particular scrutiny.

Rafe was prone to spend his nights on-the-town with his mates, most of whom like him were more 'out of' rather than 'in' work. It was on one such night that this comfortable lifestyle was dislodged forever.

They had been carousing through the streets, as was their habit, when Rafe suggested they do a make-over of the east wing entrance hall at Driffield.

'Come on, you lot. Gus an' me'll sort out Churchill's bust by the stairs, you and Denny do a job on the foot-soldiers at the "Battle of Waterloo" in that glass case over there.'

…'Now, what d'yer think?'

'What a cigar! Pervert!'

'Put yer beer on top of his 'ed, yeah?' hiccupped Rafe.

'Denny's got the glass lid off. Bang! Bang! Now the horses've copped it! Lay 'em out, man, an' turn the Brits round to beat the retreat. That's it.'

'Yeah - leg it, comrades, the Froggies are coming!'

So, a jolly night was had by all.

The Dean was not amused. The following morning Rafe, summoned to his study, was castigated for his behaviour and that of his mindless associates, and banned from the college forthwith. So, finally let loose from the fetters of his elders and betters, Rafe went on his way shaking-down with his intimates in a descending spiral of life-style that is often the tendency with those seeking an image that seems to fit.

* *

Meanwhile, Anatole had joined the protest against animal experiments at the new Bio Medical Science Buildings in South Parks Road. He was angered when an academic denounced them as 'aliens'.

'You call us aliens? I haven't seen one, but I really hope they have better morals than us.' A policeman edged him further away.

'Come on, move along.'

'END ANIMAL ABUSE,' roared Anatole through his megaphone. 'ADVANCES IN TECHNOLOGY MAKE THE TORTURING OF ANIMALS UNNECESSARY.'

'You're obstructing the traffic, move on.'

Anatole shouted even louder, 'ANIMAL EXPERIMENTS MUST STOP!'

The demonstrators picked up this slogan, and yelled it in unison through Radcliffe Square and along the High.

A junior reporter from the local daily spotted his opportunity for a scoop, and by evening a picture of Anatole grappling with a policeman attempting to confiscate his megaphone appeared with the caption *DRIFFIELD ANIMAL RIGHTS PROTESTOR CAUTIONED.* It was enough to have him likewise banned from the college, which he could not understand, having done little harm to anyone while attempting to prevent a great deal of harm in animal exploitation. So, reluctantly, he also packed his bags and set out for pastures new.

It is perhaps not surprising that the Dean and his committee arranged to re-house the Head of College Maintenance and their mother in a very small flat above the college car-park. How they missed the view of the rather beautiful quad!

* * *

# AFTER MOUTHFULS

'Did you notice that woman over there, Hilary? She's put a fiver under a bit of her scone.'

'Where?'

'She's at the till now.'

'How odd. I seem to recognise her from somewhere…but I can't think where.'

'Well, as I was saying, next Tuesday it's our group's genealogy night. You never know, I could discover I've titled ancestors. They could have perished on the Titanic - heaven forbid! Then Thursday it's parents' evening. I'm not going to bring the kids - are you going to bring yours?'

'Oh, yes, probably. I didn't know it was optional. Is Ken going?'

'He's not over-keen. I'd like him to. All depends on what sort of day he's had.'

'I know where I've seen her - the inter-school football match. She sat behind a tree!'

\* \*

It's a relief to get outside. The air is fresh. It's damp and there's a mist. That's a relief too, I prefer to be indistinct. Only a woman with a loud voice seemed to notice my hasty exit. She stopped talking briefly, looked me up and down, put me into some slot or other, then carried on, loudly, from where she'd left off.

I haven't actually been able to leave a tip in a café till today. Now I think about it, probably the easiest way to do, is, without looking, edge some coins under a saucer but even then people can guess how much you've left - and that sums you up!

I couldn't help panicking, and left my five-pound note under the half-eaten scone on the plate. I felt terrified I'd choke after that last mouthful. I just had to get away. It was my bus-fare home and now I'll have to walk. It's drizzling and there's a steep hill to climb, and my shopping. Always a steep hill; it doesn't get any easier.

Good, there's no-one about so I don't have to invent aliases or disguises to get over the crisis of being recognised. All I want is to be able to go into a café, order a pot of tea and something to eat and not feel noticed - observed among all the other people. It's when I feel exposed like that I have to resort to inventing fantasies, or rituals - whatever it takes to cope with the… predicament.

In that tea-shop I imagined I was a dwarf so I wouldn't need to see anything above the height of the table. But when I did need to and my eye was caught by the woman with the loud voice, I had this feeling I was going to choke. I switched quickly to being a bird of prey hovering way above her, my eagle eye trained on her kaleidoscopic jacket and a flower-thing in her hair. I thought, 'I'll seize it in my beak and pluck it from her head, that'll shut her up!'

That's another thing - it haunts me sometimes that I'm never sure I'm going to be able to actually swallow what's in my mouth, so it just sits there on my tongue till I bend over my handbag or something and get rid of it in my hanky. Then I tell myself I'm not alone, everyone has coping strategies of some kind to face their demons, though they're not always aware of it.

Sometimes, when it reaches breaking point, I think it might be better, easier all round, to inhabit a permanent fantasy existence and just pay lip-service to what goes on outside.

'Celia?'

There's Frank at the gate. He won't like to see me in these wet clothes.

'Coming. Are the children back from after-school club? … Hi… I missed the bus and decided to walk home. Then it started to rain… and I didn't want to bother using the mobile.'

Our eyes meet and speak volumes in the silence, and I'm drowning under his penetrating gaze. He'll guess there's been an… incident.

'Frank, you'll want your dinner - I've got the shopping here, it won't take long.'

'Yes they're indoors safe and sound. Sam's got a few bumps and bruises. Someone on the bus damaged his school cap.'

…Pl-ea-se Frank, don't say it! Don't remind me - parents' evening looming large - only a few days off.

\* \*

I persuaded Frank that he was too tired after his conference to go to the school. I hadn't bothered him with the letter requesting us to see Mr Marchent, Head-of-Year-6, on Parents' Evening at 7:45p.m. I was afraid fathers wouldn't be there apart from us and we'd stand out.

I got into a fever wracking my brain for coping strategies. They whittled down to two possible ways of disengaging myself from the whole painful situation. One was to masquerade as a CID officer and then *I* could question Mr Marchent instead of him questioning me. I'd be in the positive seat and he'd be in the negative one.

I rehearsed things to say like, 'I'll do the investigating, that's my job' and 'I'm satisfied that this person has come forward' and 'case-closed, don't you think?'

If only I knew what *he'd* be saying. Sam really likes him, tells us he always listens to a boy's point of view and he teaches P.E. as well as biology. Sam always gets good school reports, so why does Mr Marchent want to see us? Thinking about it, my idea's crazy! I'd never be able to pull it off. Just meeting him is going to be a fearful ordeal. He'd know if I had a job like that.

The only other avoidance strategy is to dwell on a happy, undemanding and relaxed time from the past, and concentrate on that. The actual situation to be faced would be merely peripheral. I'd just reply to any question that comes up when really necessary. Yes, our holiday in Ireland. Yes, the Blasket Islands off the Dingle peninsula - deserted and wild, and wonderfully peaceful. We saw seals basking and sashaying and playing in the sun. We came so close we could see their bulging eyes and curved whiskers, and they didn't mind us a bit.

* *

'Good evening, Mrs Donoghue.'

I look at an extended hand and offer mine. He shakes it and I have to look up. He's smiling and appears relaxed. I force my face into a smile.

'Take a seat. Is Mr Donoghue here?'

'No, he's not here.'

Mr Marchent is much younger than I expected - he can't be more than thirty - fair hair, athletic build, looks the rugby type, but rather charming. I sit on the edge of the chair.

'It's just - we're rather concerned about Sam. Recently he has sustained bruises on more than one occasion and we are wondering why...'

'Oh.'

*(Seals are being washed gently to-and-fro by the tide, to-and-fro.)*

'Have you asked him about it? ... Has he talked about anything unusual or out of character?...'

'Sam was injured on the school bus. He was swinging his cap, to-and-fro.'

'I don't quite understand.'

'It had manure in it.'

Mr. Marchent looks quite nonplussed and the door opens, and Frank comes in with a woman I recognise from somewhere.

'Don't worry Celia, Sam asked me to come. I must explain, Mr Marchent, that Sam had a fight on the school bus this afternoon, and it's not the first time. Apparently two boys filled his cap with…some objectionable mess. He's just pointed out one of them in the school hall and this lady is his mother. She's come to say her son's admitted doing it and she's really upset that he and another boy set upon him.'

It's the lady from the tea-shop, and she's still wearing the flower-thing in her hair.

'I'd call that bullying wouldn't you?'

Frank is surprised at my confident outburst.

'I'm satisfied that this lady has come forward and I trust a suitable punishment will be meted out. Case-closed, don't you think?'

Frank reacts with shock and awe, the head-of-year is bemused and the lady from the tea-shop is chastened, but I feel relieved and, yes, exhilarated at the way things are turning out.

I'm growing out of myself, I'm not deranged. I'm well aware of my 'avoidance personality disorder' as they call it, and *I've* been the positive one. I just had to blurt out that it was bullying, for Sam's sake. I spoke up for him.

\* \* \*

# THE SEASON 2006

*The Times* fills a gap in the day. On Sunday a little calendar of 'The Coming Season' dropped out with Veuve Clicquot Ponsardin Champagne, 'adding a thrill to the season' sketched on the cover.

'Let's see - 17th March - that's St. Patrick's Day, and it was the Gold Cup at Cheltenham National Hunt Festival,' I tell my husband.

'No saint looked out for the horses this year - they're either dead or injured,' (he's Irish so he'd know, though I don't think he bets).

Then on 2nd of April, the Oxford v. Cambridge Boat Race and the Badminton Horse Trials in May. The tennis, of course, at Wimbledon in June. It's a very busy time, for then there's Royal Ascot followed by Henley Royal Regatta. After that, the Hampton Court Palace Flower Show etc. etc., and finally Glorious Goodwood from 1st to 5th August.

Then all the well-to-do disperse abroad for holidays on yachts or exotic islands. The Queen can't go on the Royal Yacht, it's been discontinued so she'll have to hire one, but she spends the summer at Balmoral so that's alright.

I'll shut my eyes and stick a toothpick into one of the diary entries and see where *I'm* going. Oh! It's the Royal Highland Games of Braemar - 2nd of September. Oooh! Will the Queen be there? How exciting! The men all seem to wear kilts and throw great poles as far as they can. What shall I wear? It'll be chilly up there, so I think it'll be the cream wrap-around from Help the Aged over the purple two-piece I wore for Stella's wedding - I'll feel quite blue-blooded in that!

Should I wear a hat? No, perhaps not. I think the Queen only wears a headscarf.

I'll take the night sleeper and have an evening meal in the dining car at one of those tables with little glowing lamps. As we fly past the mountains and glens, I'll sip a glass of that champagne with the highfaluting name - I wish!

I look at my husband on the sofa, asleep now. He has a dried up trickle of blood on his forehead. He did that sorting out the hedges. His hand is dropping down with his paper to his knees, the dog's backside tucked up against him. His glasses are still on his nose and his other hand is hooked across his chest like a claw. He has such long fingers, the skin stretched taut across his knuckles. We're old now. We dream, we get tired, we forget things. His paper drops to the floor.

I watch him sigh deeply and reflect on how hard it is for the romantic love we had when we were young to endure over the years. The wear-and-tear of living, like everything to do with age, dulls. Repeating the day-to-day becomes the easiest and the challenge of doing something exciting and new is more readily available in dreams. Yet I love his long legs, blue eyes and weathered face. He's still handsome to me, and his concern to please and such a straight and honest life he leads. He gently snores.

After watching the highland games I'll extend my trip and catch a train south to Edinburgh, first-class of course. A uniformed waiter will bring me breakfast and the paper and as many cups of coffee as I like while I read news of what's happening in the world. Then I'll get a taxi to the five-star Balmoral Hotel and request a room directly overlooking Princes Street.

Such day-dreams remind me of a holiday at the Edinburgh Festival I had, countless years ago, with a friend. We were students. We didn't stay anywhere like the Balmoral, of course. It was a rambling kind of old house doing B & B, where they locked the door at half-past eleven. We'd been dancing at a party till the wee hours and the men had dropped us off. They helped us open the sash-window at the back and we landed on a table set for breakfast. We were giggling as we trod in the dish of marmalade and it broke!

We went to the Braque Exhibition which was on everyone's list of 'must sees'. I actually really like the Braque paintings - all those cubes and abstract shapes leave plenty to the imagination.

The main theatre event though, which everyone definitely wanted tickets for, was a Greek tragedy at the Usher Hall. Strange, I don't remember the play, only that the main characters wore huge masks with horrible gaping mouths apparently to produce a megaphone effect. I thought it was all a bit of a disappointment, but I kept that to myself.

I'll have Scotch kippers for breakfast with all the trimmings and I'll buy a pair of tartan socks at Harvey Nichols, that the men wear with their kilts, for him. I wonder, would he ever wear them? I like the Royal Stewart best with all the vivid colours.

Now I'll be one of those fortune-tellers, except I peer into the past... I see a young man watching me as I buy the socks. He grins and asks me where I'm going to wear them.

'At the dance, where I'll whirl like a top in my circular plaid skirt,' I laugh. He asks me what I'd advise him to see at the Festival.

'Not the Greek tragedy with the characters wearing ghastly megaphone masks!' I reply. Then he laughs. He has deep violet eyes, which seem to tease as I glance at him, a little embarrassed, and a rather unruly mop of curly brown hair. He asks if he can join me when I next go to the theatre. I feel so exhilarated and my pulse misses a beat because I have a feeling that something wonderful is going to happen…

The snoring stops. I reluctantly fast-forward fifty years and re-focus. He is watching me.

'What were you dreaming about?'

'Oh, nothing in particular,' I reply.

He doesn't often confide in me what he dreams about, and he wouldn't tell me about flights of fancy like mine. That isn't between us.

Dwelling, even a little while, on the passing of time is…painful. I expect the Queen will feel like that too.

* * *

# TRAVELLING THROUGH TIME

'Could I speak to a Mrs. Carole Sayer?'

'Speaking.'

'This is Constable McLoughlin from Darlington Police. I'm afraid I've some bad news, Mrs Sayer. A lady by the name of Annie Duggan has been found and declared deceased at 160 Greenbank Road. We understand from her solicitor that you are to be contacted in the event of her death. Is that correct?'

'Oh, that's dreadful! Yes … What's happened?'

'The window-cleaner saw her on the floor in the sitting-room yesterday morning. The cause of death is awaiting the post-mortem. I need to ask if you are willing to collect the keys to the house from the police station and undertake the necessary arrangements?'

'Yes, of course... I'll come... I'll have to contact my husband at work - and make provisions for the family and everything - and it'll take three hours or so to get there... Can you tell me your name again?'

'Constable Gerard McLoughlin.'

Ray checked the authenticity of the phone call and it was evening before we got to the police station. The constable was off-duty and the only news we had was that Annie's body had been moved to the mortuary. They thought she must have died the previous night, as they'd found the electric fire and TV on.

The house was exactly as it was when we last visited. Annie was always the tidiest - everything had to be in place just as her mother Aunty Kitty had it, nothing different, and she died over twenty years ago. You'd never guess that between the death of both of them Annie's husband, Henry, had come and gone, not having survived a leg amputation. No photos, no mementoes; it was as if he had never existed, and to think they'd been engaged for over ten years! Neither partner felt they could leave their mother till both mothers had - passed away - so to speak, which had scuppered any marriage plans.

The sitting-room seemed eerie. The first thing that hit me was how hot it was. We found her newspaper open at the TV page but it was dated five days earlier, so that was surely when she had died. No wonder the room was still hot; the fire must have been on for five days and nights.

When we used to visit, my attention always gravitated to the sitting-room mantelpiece which had two Doulton figurines of a lady balloon-seller - one at each end. This was because as a child I'd accidentally damaged one and it had cracked, and I always remember I was too scared to tell Aunty Kitty what I'd done. Strangely, now I noticed for the first time there was only one on the mantelpiece. I picked it up to see if it was the cracked one. It was. But then, even more strangely, my memory suddenly experienced an intensely vivid and detailed recollection of something that happened way back in the past, something buried deep in my sub-conscious which I seemed to have unearthed due to the terrible shock of Annie's death …

\* \*

'Why do we have to go to Aunt Kitty's? Why do we *have* to? Why do we have to go to Aunty …'

'Oh stop whining and get in.'

The train is packed with people, mainly in army uniform, and I struggle along the corridor,

103

my heavy suitcase strapped with Roddy's trouser-belt because the locks don't work and the hinges are rusty. I try to keep up with Mum and Jess, stumbling over the kit-bags of the soldiers. Flicking their cigarettes, they drop ash on my head.

'No seats, all the carriages are full,' Mum shouts over her shoulder. We can't find any standing room with enough space to put down our cases. We struggle on till we get to the lavatory at the end of the corridor, then there's a space. Soldiers one after another are pushing the door in and pulling it to get out, and each time a slot goes from 'vacant' to 'engaged' there is a horrid smell every time it's vacant. My sandwiches are squashed and I've lost my bottle of milk and Jess won't share hers.

The air-raid siren sounds. Its wailing noise must have jerked the engine to wake up 'cause steam shoots up and hisses past the window. Doors slam, then there's a whistle, and the train seems to get scared 'cause it suddenly shudders and bursts out into the dark with the load of people.

I perch on my suitcase, turning my feet in so the men can't tread on them. Mum and Jess are perched on theirs, like birds, on the other side of the door.

Through the window searchlights stare at bombed-out houses. They don't stand up properly, just great lumps of walls and heaps of rubble and cinders and piles of burnt wood and ash all over the place. There must have been some ginormous bonfire nights. It's so creepy! All those rows of bone shapes with skulls stare across the tracks, their window-eyes gone, and sometimes bits of cloth like lashes flutter as our train steams past. Every dead home is a ghost caught in the searching light, and then it's suddenly black.

Soldiers drink beer, laughing and swearing. They have bands on their arms with 'C - a - t - t - e - r - i - c - k' written on them. The ticket pinned on my chest says 'Darlington'… The toilet door opens and closes… Vàcant-engàged, vàcant-engàged … the train rocks… I'm tired … vàcant-engàged …  vàcant …

The sky is grey and ugly. It's very cold. We sit on Aunt Kitty's front doorstep - on news-papers the soldiers had left behind. Mummy says it's too early to knock and get them up. I wish we could go home, even if doodle-bugs do come.

'Mum, I want to go home… It's horrible here. Mum… I'll run away if we can't go home.'

First she pretends she hasn't heard me, then she suddenly gets up. She's cross. She starts to shake me.

'Why can't you be quiet!? I've had enough of you. Jess isn't making a scene like you.'

'It's always Jess! She's older than me, and she wouldn't share her milk with me. I'm so cold I want to die.' I'm desperate. I shout to Aunt Kitty's window, 'THIS IS LIKE ALL THE DEAD HOUSES.' Mum gives me a clout. 'Ouch! OUCH!' …

\* \*

Yes, it hurt - I remember because my mother had never hit me like that before or since; it's something a child never forgets. Ironically, now this is truly a dead house.

There were a lot of things I learnt about Annie as we cleared it out. She was broad and solid, and a predictable person. But among her possessions, tucked away and never worn, was a flimsy pink nightdress with bows and ribbons, and a beige lace-embroidered camisole and undies, and a dark-coloured wig of ringlets and a fringe. Oh, Annie, what dreams did you once have? And all my memory is of how I hated staying at Aunty Kitty's and you so dominating and bossy. When I aimed Bobby the budgie's mirror at you, it missed and cracked this Doulton figurine – Annie, I'm so sorry. Oh, Annie…

\* \* \*

# AUNTIE LOU

His voice was reaching its crescendo.

'They're bastards! Absolute bastards! I'll not have you going around with those toffee-nosed malingerers and getting the worse for drink at your age.'

Lois's face reddened. She didn't want them to see her from the kitchen but she couldn't do anything about the door gaping wide.

'They're nothing on your lousy friends - they're a bunch of freaks and losers.'

She eased further down the sofa to better hide behind the presents piled under the tree and, drawing her bag of parcels closer, she set about checking the contents.

Roddy, her eldest nephew, the object of his father's wrath, was - oh dear - to get *The Moonstone* by Wilkie Collins, and, worse still, Mark Twain's *The Adventures of Tom Sawyer and Huckleberry Finn* (which are now considered racist). She realised they were quite unsuitable - at fourteen he seemed so grown-up, and taking on his father like that, without batting an eyelid! She panicked and started to rummage in her coat pockets for her wallet.

He'll want money - it's probably what they'll all want. Maybe not Margo; she'd watched Margo through the glazed front-door (you waited forever for anyone to answer the bell if the dog didn't hear) walking down the hall rocking a doll to and fro in her arms with a dummy in its mouth. Amazingly it burped and cried and tears rolled down its cheeks. Changing the dummy for a bottle she then walked up the hall and it gurgled and made rude noises. Yes, Margo will be alright with the nurse's outfit, she decided with relief.

'Don't use that kind of language - and we're not talking about me, we're talking about a policeman coming to this house last night over an incident outside McDonald's.'

She counted out the contents of her wallet: four ten-pound notes and four fives. That meant twenty pounds each for Roddy, Niall and Euan, and left her with some small change. She quickly pulled the wrapping off the books and hid them behind the sofa. Conveniently, the money could go inside their Christmas cards.

'But it wasn't us. They know our school types and wanted a punch-up and our stuff.'

'How? You weren't wearing any uniform.'

'They know… Oh, I don't know… You know… The way we talk, our designer gear 'n stuff. You should be pleased - Leo got his mobile out so fast, the police were round in six minutes. They'd pulled a knife, but we ran into a shop and they got the wind up and went.'

There was a long pause. She raised her head and peeped into the kitchen. There seemed to be a stand-off. They were glowering at each other.

'Whatever about that, Roddy, as far as those boys are concerned, you're grounded for the rest of Christmas.'

'They're my mates!'

'They're not your mates - they're just over-moneyed, idle lay-a-bouts. They're not doing you, or the school, any favours.'

…Silence. Things seemed to be calming down a bit. She'd make her presence known in a minute.

Her eyes strayed through the bay-window to the Trust Grounds beyond the garden. High up in the Monterey pines, ring-necked parakeets were screeching and shooting from tree to tree. They were early nesters and already searching to take-over holes made by woodpeckers. Such exotic birds, so striking with their pea-green feathers and scarlet beaks, like brash young bucks - like Roddy.

The other book in her carrier-bag was the *RSPB Handbook of British Birds* for Niall, her favourite nephew. He's interested in birds, but of course he'll expect money, to be like the others, and she pulled off the 'For Niall, with love' tag. It could be a family present. Euan wouldn't want it - he's too young and doesn't read much unless he has to. She'd got puzzles for him, but they could be family presents too.

She stood up quickly as they came out of the kitchen and put on her broad smile.

'Margo answered the door; she's just gone to put her doll to bed.'

'Lois, welcome! I didn't hear the bell, give me your coat. How's things? I haven't seen you since…would you believe it, since last Christmas. You look well.'

'Yes, I'm well. And how's Roddy? My, how you've grown!'

'I'm OK, Auntie Lou… Mum's arranged a buffet in the dining-room…in your honour - and for the other kids, Niall's and Euan's mates.' He glanced at Hugh. 'Dad and I haven't got any on tap that are suitable.' Hugh cut in quickly.

'Jeanette's doing the home-run to collect everyone. Come and have a glass of sherry, Lois. They'll be back shortly.'

The buffet supper wasn't the organised round-the-table gathering they'd had in previous years. Now what happens, as far as the children are concerned, is you put a bit of everything you want on a big plate and take it to the lounge, plug your ears with your Walkman or iPod or some such. You eat while beating out syncopated rhythms on your knee with spoons, or banging your head in time with them against the back of the chair, or the wall. The alternative is to go in the TV room and watch aliens and terror on a big screen.

Lois was three years older than her sister Jeanette, who always used to be the one to organise the get-together - if she set her mind to it. She had a lovely voice and was invariably primed to sing 'Mary's Boy Child' and 'Eden Was Just Like This' at Christmas, the Harry Belafonte equivalents of today's 'number one'. Lois would accompany her on the piano.

Both sisters were considered attractive, but Jeanette, with her greenish eyes and auburn wayward curls was the clever, outgoing one, but somehow too inattentive to find a niche for her talents. Lois, on the other hand, had dark hair framing her face and persevered quietly in harnessing her flair in Fine Art.

Last year she had given the children a one-for-all present - a keyboard synthesiser, which she had found to be breathtaking. It brought back all the childhood memories. Their brother Robert would start things off with his mouth-organ rendering of Vera Lynn's 'We'll Meet

Again'. Then Dad would rise to the challenge and play to Mum the only tune he could manage with a comb and paper – 'Two Lovely Black Eyes, Oh What a Surprise'. However, before supper when she went to the bathroom, which was being renovated, *there* was the keyboard amongst other stuff in the bath, covered with plaster-dust!

After Jeanette had cleared away the 'cold table' (her name for the buffet), she said she'd get the children to organise a game in the dining-room. Margo was particularly excited.

'We'll call you all in when we've planned what to do,' she confided to her aunt.

'Sherry, Lois?' Hugh asked as he rolled his brandy balloon over the Christingle candle which Margo got from school, and insisted on re-igniting for 'atmosphere'.

'Yes, thank you,' he poured himself a brandy in the warmed glass. 'How's the work going?'

'Oh, I've a few commissions in the pipe-line - posters advertising exhibitions and suchlike.'

'Sounds fascinating,' Jeanette interposed. 'Must be very relaxing to have a flair like that you can always rely on and no-one to distract you,' she said, glancing at Hugh. 'I so envy you Lois. You know I've often thought you were wrong to give up your partner-ship with Ben. You were both so similar in your tastes and so suited to each other. I believed it would be a real success in every way, you know?'

'But you see, he was married.'

'Yes, I know, but…'

'Let it be,' Hugh intervened.

Margo barged in, hopping from one foot to the other, her face all flushed.

'Who's going to play "Blind Man's Bluff"? … Auntie Lou, you're going to be first.'

'Buff.'

'Pardon?'

'It's called "Blind Man's Buff"' Jeanette said.

'Roddy said "Bluff".'

'He would,' said Hugh, dryly.

'Anyway, you've got to be "it", Auntie Lou, and we blindfold you with my scarf.'

'What do I do?'

'The boys have made up a special version. I'll tell you.'

Lois felt doubtful about the boys' special version. She had a sense of unease about even going in for the game at all. Things seem to have changed so much now. The children growing up so fast, and growing away from how it was, from how it used to be.

Outside the dining-room door, her sense of unease grew into something of a panic. They could be capable of anything when they'd blindfolded her and she'd be completely at their mercy. She tried to imagine what they might do, how far they might go. She had recollections of a game that went too far. The boy who played "it" was blindfolded and his hands were tied behind his back. He had to wear a mask and be a kind of totem-pole. The players then danced round and round and prodded the 'totem' with sticks, chanting to beats of a drum and it became more and more frenetic. The victim was then made to kneel over a bucket of water with an apple floating in it and he had to get it with his mouth before the blindfold could be removed. He nearly suffocated.

Margo was reading to the boys from an exercise book.

'I'm the black witch Miss Eumenides Poison. My skill is to deliver Justice, and this is my black blindfold. My cloak and everything about me is black. You are my Furies and are thirsty for revenge, but I am more kindly than you.'

Lois had heard enough.

'Margo, I'm sorry, I haven't time to play the game right now. In fact, there'll be so much traffic on the roads and crowds of people doing their last minute shopping, I'll have to consider making tracks.'

'Oh, Auntie Lou, you can't chicken-out now, we're all ready for you.'

'I'm so sorry Margo. How about asking your dad to take my place?'

'He won't. He knows we'll do something awful and yucky, and get in a mood.'

'Well, how about a game with each other? What about "Goodies and Baddies"?'

'It won't be the same as making you go through my Cave of Demons.'

'Well, maybe it can be a special game to save for later in the holiday, don't you think Margo?' She just winced at her aunt's betrayal, but Lois had not recovered from the shock of it all and her attention was catapulted to the problem of how to get away, and how to get home with only a few coins in her purse and her return ticket.

'Do you think your mother could give me a lift to the station?' she asked Niall, who was now coming out of the dining-room with the other boys. By this time Margo had burst off to get her doll out of bed and give her a feed.

'Sure thing, she's not been drinking like dad 'cause she's doing the home-run anyway. Party's over guys - Mum'll give you a lift home. Mum!' He shouted.

'Oh, is the "Blind Man's Bluff" over? That's rather sudden, isn't it?' said Jeanette, coming out of the lounge with her brandy balloon.

\* \* \*

# TAIL END

'Hello, Maggie - what's it to be?'

'Where's Gus?'

'Look, I haven't time for conversation now - there's customers waiting. I'll get you your usual and join you in a minute.'

She snatches the Becks, eyes him coldly and slams some coins on the counter. She stares through the window till her eyes fix on a cottage at the other side of the green, its roof charred, its dormer gone. Eventually the barman indicates an empty chair and gets a stool for himself. He takes a cloth from his belt, hesitates, then wipes the table. He's tense, wiping in broad sweeps, not quite knowing how to begin.

'He's... left you, Maggie. Came with his backpack, downed his double-on-the-rocks and said he's catching the 'Farewell to Arms'.'

'What's that mean?'

'You tell me…living together I guess. He's left you a dog.'

'What dog?'

'It's a lurcher. It's out in the yard at the back.'

'What for?'

'It's a nice dog. He says it's called "Whistle-in-the-Wind".'

'Are you being funny? What have you two been plotting? It's crazy, what you're saying.'

'No, you two are the crazies. It's nothing to do with me. All I know is you've come to the end of the line, Maggie - the drinking and fighting. Torching the house was beyond the pale. Why did you do that? Gus was brought up in that house. It's in a grim state now, and he's had enough. He's taken off - for good.'

She says nothing for a long time, then mutters, 'why did he leave me a dog?'

'I don't know…he couldn't give you kids… I can only guess it's to leave you something to… love, if you can, if you're able, otherwise it's on its own whistling in the wind.'

'It's his sick joke.'

'He wasn't joking, that's for sure. Look, Maggie, you've got half a house that's still habitable and Whistle-in-the-Wind; that's what you've got, and it's better than a cardboard box from some draughty underpass in the middle of nowhere. It's closing time, so I'll get the dog from the back, OK?'

'It's his sick joke.'

The dog ambles in, tail between its legs turned up at the end, willing enough to obey the lead as if it doesn't mind not knowing what to expect. The clock is ticking …

'You'll be "Luke", not some screwball son-of-a-bitch name. I'll keep my eye open for the cardboard box,' she mutters over her shoulder.

* * *